Banned In Boston

A Slightly Naughty-But-Nice
Fable of the 1980s

Dedicated to the writers who made us laugh
and helped us find our own voices:

Woody Allen, Russell Baker, Erma Bombeck,
Mel Brooks, Art Buchwald, Nora Ephron, Jules Feiffer,
Stan Freberg, Elaine May, Mike Nichols, Barbara Pym,
Carl Reiner, Robert Sheckley, Shel Silverstein,
Neil Simon, James Thurber,
and so many others.

Banned In Boston

A Slightly Naughty-But-Nice
Fable of the 1980s

Deborah Hand-Cutler
and Daniel M. Kimmel

BLACK HORSE PRESS
TEHACHAPI · CALIFORNIA

ISBN 13: 9781736516508

Cover Design by Terri Asher

Black Horse Press

Preface

Daniel Kimmel and Deborah Hand lived in apartments in the same small building in Boston's Back Bay during the 1980s. While chatting in the laundry room one day, they discovered they were both writers and film buffs. Dan and Debby began to frequent the nearby Nickelodeon Theatre together. The "Nick" was Boston's mecca for independent films not making the rounds of the major theaters, and the two friends became regular patrons.

Neither Dan nor Debby ever ventured down to the Combat Zone for movies, however – at least not that they would ever admit to each other. They did once take their umbrellas to a midnight showing of *The Rocky Horror Picture Show*, which was playing in one of Boston's venerable old theaters down the street from them.

Just for fun, they tried their hand at writing a screenplay together, which they called *Banned in Boston*. When Deborah had to move back to California for family reasons, however, the script went with her.

Life occupied both of them for the next thirty years. Daniel became a film critic and wrote Science Fiction and humor. Deborah became a musician and a local politician in Tehachapi, California. She also wrote essays for the local newspapers on music and politics.

While in the pandemic lockdown of 2020, Deborah decided to make an archeological dig into a row of filing cabinets along the back wall of her garage. One of the artifacts that was unearthed from the rubble was the script of *Banned in Boston*, written so many years ago.

Dan and Debby, having renewed their friendship online, decided that what we need after the trauma of 2020 is a bit of silliness from a bygone era. The 1980s are not so long ago, really, but long enough to feel like an age of innocence. They decided to make a novel out of their old screenplay.

If you're new to Boston, this book can act as a bit of a travel guide. If you're a former or present long-time resident, it might bring back some nostalgic memories of the way we were not so long ago.

Banned In Boston

A Slightly Naughty-But-Nice
Fable of the 1980s

"Things are not always what they seem."

Prologue

A long time ago, in a somewhat mythical town called Boston, there was this thing known as "standards." The word is rarely used today, and even less understood. Even then, way back in the mid-1980s, there was wide confusion over what it meant.

When it came to the entertainment media, Boston had been in the forefront of those bemoaning the lack of standards on stage, in books and in the movies. The "Bluenoses" of old in the city particularly railed against the evils of burlesque in the old Scollay Square Red Light District.

That area was demolished in the early 1960s to make way for the new Government Center. Many of the Scollay Square establishments relocated to a run-down section on lower Washington Street that became known as the Combat Zone. The name honored visiting soldiers and sailors who often frequented the area in uniform for a drink and friendly fistfight.

This part of Boston was already an entertainment district, and included some of the old movie palaces, as well as bars and restaurants known for their "after-dark" activities. Some of the theaters that could only afford to show second-run films began offering "porno flicks" to their more discerning customers.

As all these changes were happening in the city, there was a lull in the fight to reclaim the purity of our souls as that horror called television became the new object of scrutiny. However, it was hard to claim that a medium offering *Ed Sullivan* and *The Beverly Hillbillies* was going to mean the end of Western civilization. At least not from depravity.

But in 1966, all hell broke loose when the United States Supreme Court ruled – in a case brought in Massachusetts, naturally – that the book, *Fanny Hill*, could not be adjudged obscene because it wasn't, in the Court's words, "utterly without redeeming social value." One didn't need a law degree to see that ANYTHING could have SOME "redeeming social value," even if nothing more than serving as a bad example. The floodgates were opened, and a new generation of "standards" defenders went into battle.

Then, in 1974, the Massachusetts Supreme Judicial Court ruled the state's obscenity laws to be unconstitutional. In the hope of containing the virus of such vices to one location and keeping it from spreading across the town, the city declared the Combat Zone the "Adult Entertainment District." Now, it became Boston's answer to "porno chic."

The next decade brought forth the VCR, and dirty movies became available at local video stores. The Combat Zone was deprived of its corner on the porno market, and Boston's antipornography groups lost their central target. Times had clearly changed.

In some ways, it now looks like a time of relative innocence, before the internet swept in and took the genre to a much deeper, darker place. Before that, for most people, stag films were just punchlines for late-night comics and talk show hosts. In any case, the business back then was something that involved "adults only," with parents doing what they could to keep it out of the hands and eyes of their teenage boys.

Although our story uses porno movies as its MacGuffin, this book is not R-rated and does include some bits of moral message along the way. However, it probably wouldn't be suitable for high school English classes – but you never know these days. The authors are simply pointing out, in what they hope is an entertaining way, that things are not always what they seem.

So now, let's go back to that simpler time in the mid-1980s and begin our story.

Chapter 1

B enjamin Porter was in love with the world today. He liked his new job. He had done all right at the 7-Eleven over the last two years, but being an Executive Director sounded better on a resume than Assistant Manager in charge of the Slurpee Machine. He finished tying his tie, put on his sport coat, tied his New Balance running shoes extra tightly, and headed out.

He grabbed the railing at the top of the stairs outside the door to his rent-controlled apartment and bounded down the four flights to the street. He touched down only eight times, at each landing and half landing. He might be close to thirty, he thought, but he was still in shape, even if he couldn't quite afford the Back Bay Racquet Club.

Ben was glad to see that Jack was behind the counter at the Charles Street 7-Eleven. He considered Jack a friend, but still liked the fact that Jack was a little jealous of Ben's new position.

"Morning Jack. How's it going? I just have time for coffee. Gotta get to the office."

He picked up a *Boston Herald* and put it on the counter so he could read as he poured himself a cup of coffee.

Jack was working nights, and his shift was almost

over. It had been a particularly boring night, and he was not in the best of moods.

"Hmph! Big Deal Executive! If I'd been on the morning shift that day, he would have offered ME the job."

"But you weren't and I was. And you also didn't have a brother-in-law who could help him file for non-profit status. So now I'M the Executive Director of Decency and Morality Now!"

"I'm supposed to be impressed!" said Jack.

Ben gave him a smug, self-satisfied look, then opened his newspaper to the Arts section. He dropped a few packets of sugar and some cream in his coffee, gave it a quick stir and gulped down half the cup.

"Why'd you want to get involved with a bunch of book burners, anyway?" Jack asked sharply.

"They're not as bad as all that, and it pays better than this job. Besides, their hearts are in the right place. Look what we're up against."

Turning to the film pages of the paper, Ben pushed it toward the other side of the counter so Jack could see a large ad for a triple-X-rated double feature.

"*Snow White and the Seven Deviants* with *Puss in Boots*," Ben read, snapping his forefinger in the middle of the ad for emphasis.

"Where's that playing?" Jack asked, only half-joking as he grabbed the paper from Ben.

"Aw, c'mon, Jack. You don't go for that stuff."

Jack released his hold on the paper.

"Nah, but it doesn't bother me. Hell, we sell worse

stuff than that right here," he said, gesturing toward the magazine rack.

Ben drained his cup of coffee and jumped off the stool.

"Correction. YOU sell it. I'M an executive. And I'm late!"

He threw some change on the counter and ran out. Jack looked after him for a moment, then picked up the paper Ben had left behind. Ben ran back in, grabbed the paper and was out the door again.

The morning commuters were beginning to clog Charles Street, jockeying for position like runners in the early minutes of a 10K. Playing a version of the favorite Boston sport of "Dodge the Cars," Ben crossed the street and headed toward the Common. The first signs of spring were apparent – the barest hint of pale yellow-green on the tips of the trees, crocuses popping up through the last remnants of soot-blackened snow. Ben was in too much of a hurry to notice. He broke into a run, across the Common by the tennis courts, and on over to Boylston Street.

Franklin Abbott didn't notice the new spring, either, although he was particularly fond of this time of year. But today he was preoccupied with other matters. He sat silently in the back of a cab as it carried him away from Beacon Hill toward the financial district. Into his contemplation, however, drifted the voice of District Attorney Burton Halloran, emanating from the cab's radio.

"When I see these movies and magazines, which degrade both women AND men, I'm embarrassed that such things are for sale in my city. But what can I do? Every time we go to court, the pornographers are back on the street the next day selling something else."

Shaking his head in disgusted agreement, Franklin looked absently out the window of the cab as they wound through the pedestrians on State Street and pulled up in front of one of the old, solid-looking office buildings wedged between the flashy glass high-rises of the district. He got out and paid the driver. After adjusting his impeccably tailored topcoat, he entered the building.

Across town in Southie – as the locals call South Boston – Margaret O'Leary knew it was spring, like she knew everything else that went on within earshot of any of her rather large circle of friends and relations. But she wouldn't count it as one of the Important Matters of the day, certainly not on a par with helping her friend Rose's next-door neighbor's sister-in-law out of a jam.

Margaret held the phone under her chin with the finesse of a concert violinist as she finished pouring her morning coffee, took the toast out of the toaster and buttered it, then sat down to serious business.

She was in her element.

"Well, or course! What are friends for? ... I'll call my nephew Jimmy down at City Hall and he'll take care of it ... No problem at all ... Besides, it's just like you said. How could Doris have seen the hydrant when it was under four feet of snow at the time ... Listen, speaking of time, it's getting late. I've got to run. I'm due at the office at 9:30 ... Don't worry. Jimmy will take care of everything."

Ben ran off the Common at the corner of Tremont and Boylston Streets. He jogged in place a few steps until he could weave through the stalled traffic and cross Boylston. Halfway down the block, he started to enter an old six-story office building but noticed Margaret inside, waiting for the elevator. He jogged in place outside, watching through the glass doors as she entered the elevator. When he saw the doors close behind her, he ran into the building and leaped up the adjoining stairs, three at a time.

The old elevator was not quite at the second-floor when Ben hit the landing. He punched the elevator button as he passed by to race up the next flight of stairs. The door opened seconds behind him, and Margaret, the lone occupant, quizzically stared out into the empty hallway.

Ben continued racing up the stairs and punching the buttons. With each floor, he put more time between himself and the elevator. Margaret was getting more and more annoyed as the elevator door opened at each and every landing for mystery riders who didn't have the common decency to show themselves.

When Ben reached the top floor, grinning ear-to-ear, he took a hard left without breaking stride and ran down to the end of the hall. His keys were now in his hand. He reached the last door on the right, unlocked it, and ran inside, shutting the door behind him.

It took him only seconds to get his jacket off, toss it on a coatrack in the corner, drop himself into a chair behind the large worktable, and spread his newspaper out. When Margaret entered the office, she was greeted by the perfect picture of her young Executive Director already on the job.

"Good morning, Margaret."

"Make a note to call the building manager. Something seems to be wrong with the elevator."

Chapter 2

"Good morning, Mr. Abbott. Mr. Bloom is expecting you. Go right in."

Franklin returned the receptionist's courtesy with a slight bow and "thank you" before passing through the plush foyer into the wood-paneled office of Leo Bloom, CPA. Balding, pudgy, and probably born middle-aged, Leo rose and shook hands with Franklin.

"So, how do we stand, Leo?"

"I've finished going over the D.A.M.N.! books ... I'm sorry I meant Decency and Morality ..."

Franklin dismissed it with a wave of his hand. The name was a tired joke that had been played on them. Unfortunately, it couldn't easily be rectified.

"Never mind. What's the bottom line?"

Leo adjusted his glasses, looked at the papers in front of him, then up at his client. Franklin exhaled a deep breath in anticipation of the doom to come.

"The bottom line is that your personal financial donations have been keeping the organization alive for over a year. If you close up shop today, in about six months I can get you in good enough shape to be able to declare bankruptcy."

"Is it really as bad as all that?"

"It's worse."

Franklin's next exhale turned into a sigh.

"I guess decency and morality just aren't marketable these days."

The one-room office of Decency and Morality Now! was equipped with furniture that had seen better days. Margaret and Ben were sitting at the large conference table that dominated the bay window area. As they discussed a New Direction for the organization over their fourth cups of coffee, Franklin entered, glum from his visit to the accountant.

"Good morning, Franklin," said Margaret, greeting him cheerfully, oblivious as always of his mood.

Franklin acknowledged her greeting with a slight nod of the head in his usual, formal way.

"Margaret, Ben."

"Ben was just talking about starting a new project," Margaret chirped.

"Something that will arouse our membership, that they can all participate in," Ben added.

Ben actually had no idea what that could possibly be, but he obviously had Margaret on the hook, so he was playing his line out for all it was worth. Franklin, however, wasn't biting today.

"I've just come from a meeting with our accountant,"

he told them. "I'm afraid there aren't going to be any more projects."

"What?" Margaret practically yelled, while Ben suddenly looked nervous.

"We're on the verge of bankruptcy," Franklin stated, actually showing the slightest bit of emotion in his voice.

"But how can that be?" pleaded Margaret. "What about our fundraising appeal? That nice man from Virginia told us that his letter would bring in thousands of dollars!"

"It did," said Franklin, sitting down at the table across from her. "But what that nice man from Virginia neglected to tell us was that his FEE would be thousands of dollars."

"You mean we just broke even?" asked Ben.

He was starting to sweat with the effort of putting the vision of himself back behind the counter at the 7-Eleven out of his head. Franklin gave him a pitying look.

"WE owe HIM three hundred dollars."

"But that's outrageous!" yelled Ben, mentally serving up a cherry Slurpee.

"Franklin," said Margaret coyly, "couldn't you ..."

"I've already paid it, Margaret," sighed Franklin, "but it's time to face facts. I simply can't keep bailing D.A.M.N.! out."

Margaret winced at Franklin's use of the acronym.

"Must you use that abbreviation? Every time I think of that lawyer McNerney ..."

"Please, let's not go there!" said Ben, cutting her off. "I gave Franklin my brother-in-law's name when I was at my last job. You wanted to incorporate as a non-profit and not have to pay Franklin's high-priced lawyer to do it. Ernie did it free of charge, at least, as a personal favor to me."

"Some favor," growled Margaret.

"How was I supposed to know you hadn't picked a name yet for your organization, that you let Ernie do it. You signed the papers he prepared. You saw what he called it. Why didn't you stop it then?"

"Because MY mind doesn't work like that. Decency and Morality Now! Indeed!"

"Friends, friends," Franklin pleaded. "We have to face facts. We're broke."

After a moment of actual silence, Ben rose and started pacing in front of the bay window that offered a view of the BeauX Arts Cinema across the street. This was cue enough for Margaret to end the oppressive quiet.

"It doesn't seem right. Everything we do turns out sour. Remember that bake sale?"

"Unfortunately, I can't forget it," said Franklin. "We raised thirty dollars and ended up creating more publicity for that depraved baker in Somerville who sells suggestive strudel. I didn't even know you could bake cakes in those shapes. He got a big write-up in the paper, and we got two lines at the end of HIS story."

"Didn't the just open up a second store in Cambridge?" asked Ben, still gazing out the window.

"Hmph!" added Margaret. "The wages of sin ..."

"Yeah," Ben agreed, while frantically searching his mind for some idea, anything, that could keep the organization going, and, not insignificantly, his job.

"Look at them down there," he thought out loud. "The BeauX Arts doesn't have any problems with money."

His brain cells finally locked onto one random thought. He turned to face the others.

"What time is it?"

Franklin glanced at his watch.

"Eleven o'clock. Why?"

"At six bucks a ticket, the BeauX Arts took in more than a hundred bucks just while I was standing here."

"It's a crime!" shrieked Margaret, enraged by the idea. "And what's worse, if we picketed the theater, they'd make even more money!"

"It does seem to work that way," said Franklin, shaking his head.

"It's scandalous!" Margaret responded, off on a roll. "We succeeded in shutting down only one film in the last five years. Three days later, it reopened. And it's STILL playing!"

"Too bad we didn't have a piece of that film," said Ben, not entirely joking. "All that money could have been pouring into our coffers."

"Now there's a lovely idea," Margaret shot back. "Why don't you get some French postcards and sell them down at the school yard while you're at it!"

"Two bits a card wouldn't take us very far," said Ben with a laugh.

Margaret was now on the verge of losing it.

"I suppose we should make our own dirty movie. There's a great fundraising idea!"

"It certainly would get us back on our feet," said Franklin, overlooking Margaret's tone of sarcasm.

Ben turned and looked Franklin in the eye, surprised the proper Boston Brahmin would actually swallow the bait.

"Are you serious, Franklin?"

"Why not?" said Franklin, returning his stare. "We'd be fighting fire with fire. When you stop to think about it, it's almost poetic justice. The very souls infected by this filth would be paying us to provide the cure."

"Now wait a minute, you two!" Margaret jumped in. "It may make SOME sense when you put it like that, but it still doesn't sound right."

"What's wrong with it?" Franklin asked her.

"It's a very cute idea," said Ben, "but you've overlooked one thing. There's no great profit in single films. They call it the porno plague because they have to produce tons of it to make a profit. Certainly, you're not suggesting we do that."

"Of course not," said Franklin. "Still, there are some individual films that make a great deal of money."

Margaret was getting more and more agitated by the conversation. Nevertheless, she did have her practical side.

"And how are we supposed to guess just which

movie will have them lining up in the street to throw their hard-earned dollars to the devil?" she asked.

Franklin smiled for the first time today.

"Why, that's simple, my dear lady. You said it yourself. It's the one WE raise a protest against."

Chapter 3

The offices of Ernest J. McNerney, Esq., were by any-one's definition, tacky. The décor proudly displayed the latest in plastic, aluminum, and phony paneling. Jeanette, the bottle blond receptionist at the outer office, was what your mother would call "cheap."

Jeanette was in the middle of painting her long, pointy nails bright raspberry when the phone rang. She was not about to quit her more important work for some-thing as mundane as answering the phone, particularly when it was probably not even for her. But on the fourth ring, a voice boomed from the inner office.

"Jeanette! You wanna get that?"

Jeanette's ample chest heaved up and down in exasperation.

"Aw right, aw RIGHT!"

She screwed the lid back on her nail polish bottle and picked up the phone with the palm of her hand.

"Good muhnin'. Atuhney McNuhney's office," she offered, in textbook Bostonese, her r's FedExed to France and replaced with a ubiquitous "huh."

Upon confirmation of her suspicions that the call was not for her, she turned her head toward the inner office, and without bothering to cover the mouthpiece of the phone, yelled:

"Ehnie!!"

"Yeah?" boomed the agitated voice from the other side of the door.

"Ya gotta phone call!"

"USE THE INTERCOM!"

Jeanette looked down at the array of buttons on the phone console.

"Oh, yeah. I fuhgot."

She found one that looked right, pressed it carefully with her fingertip, avoiding her nail, and leaned into the voice box.

"Ehnie, ya gotta phone call."

Jeanette jumped in her chair at the wonder of it all as Ernie's voice came back over the intercom.

"Who is it?"

"Just a second."

She turned her attention back to the phone.

"Who is it?"

Then she pushed the intercom button again in triumph!

"It's ya brothuh-in-law. You wanna speak to him or should I tell him yo-ah out?"

"Did you put him on hold?" asked the voice from the intercom.

Jeanette looked down at the phone console.

"Naw."

"So he just heard you ask me if I was in?" asked the intercom voice.

Jeanette looked at the receiver in her hand and then at the intercom.

"Yeah, I guess so."

A sigh came back to her through the intercom.

"All right, Jeanette, I'll talk to him."

Franklin and Margaret had just carried their coffee to the table at The Coffee Connection when Ben came over and sat down in the booth.

"He'll see us at three o'clock today."

"I don't like it," said Margaret in a half-whisper. If word gets out about this we're ruined!"

"He can't tell anyone," Ben said, trying to reassure her. "It's like with a priest or a doctor. It's privileged information. He could lose his license."

"But what if he ..."

"Excuse me, Margaret," said Franklin under his breath like a bad guy in a Bogart movie. "I think we should continue this conversation somewhere else."

"We could go back to the office," Ben suggested.

"Not until they fix that elevator!" Margaret protested, as Franklin looked puzzled.

"It's such a nice morning," said Ben. "I know just the place."

The three soldiers for Decency and Morality Now!

22

quickly finished their coffees, then left the restaurant and marched across the Common to the Public Garden. Although this was the first day above forty-five degrees since November, the Garden was still deserted except for the city gardeners planting tulips and daffodils in the flowerbeds.

Ben led Margaret and Franklin to the dock at the edge of the duck pond. It was still too early in the year for the crews to start repainting the swan boats, so the three conspirators could sit on a bench on the dock with the total assurance that no one was eavesdropping.

Franklin gave a furtive glance over each shoulder, just in case.

"It is a lovely day," Franklin said, to cover his nervousness.

Margaret, as usual in times like these, was simply annoyed.

"To think I'd live to see the day where I'd come to the Public Garden to talk about making a dirty ...."

"Now, Margaret," Franklin replied. "We've gone over this ...."

"I know, I know. But why do we have to deal with this slimy McNerney? Why can't we just do it ourselves?"

"Ernie's the only person we can go to in confidence who has the contacts to help us out," Ben answered.

"How can we trust him?" Margaret shot back. "He DEFENDS these people!"

"That's precisely why we need his help. If we were to deal with the filmmakers directly ..."

"And do you REALLY want to meet them?" Franklin asked.

"Sooner or later, someone would figure out who we are," Ben added.

"And heaven forbid Mother should ever find out. Look, Margaret, just because these people are shameless doesn't mean they're idiots. Someone seeing us make the movie and then protesting it is bound to put two and two together."

"Now, there's a pretty thought, Franklin. What would happen if we got caught?" Margaret asked, with indignation.

"You mean besides the public humiliation?" Franklin responded.

He and Margaret both turned to Ben, who shifted uneasily on the bench before answering.

"Well, there's always the outside chance we could end up in jail."

"Jail?!" Margaret exclaimed, looking at him in horror. "Why would we go to jail?"

"We're going to have to raise money from our members to organize the fight to ban this movie."

"Why?" asked Franklin.

"Because it's going to look suspicious if we don't," said Ben. "Once we get the ball rolling, we'll want to get the film into court to have it declared obscene, right?"

"Of course," said Franklin. "But we'll lose. We always do. That's what we're counting on."

"And that's fraud," said Ben. "It's raising money under false pretenses."

"Do they send people to jail just for that?" Margaret asked.

"They do if they catch you at it," Ben said. "That's why we need Ernie. As long as he's fronting for us, there's no chance anyone will figure out who's behind it."

"All right, all right," said Margaret, giving in. "If only we weren't so desperate. I just don't like that McNerney."

"Think of the fight we'll be able to put up once we're solvent again," said Franklin, trying to keep himself convinced. "Our film might be the last dirty movie ever shown in Boston."

"Franklin is right," said Ben. "Let's just leave everything to Ernie. He'll help us out. He's a reasonable man."

Chapter 4

"I'm sorry, but this is really TOO good!"

Attorney Ernie McNerney was laughing so hard his cigar ashes were flying all over his desk.

"Let me get this straight. You want to make a dirty movie to help you fight dirty movies," Ernie repeated, wiping tears from his eyes.

Franklin, true to his patrician upbringing, was perfectly composed, while Margaret was preoccupied with visions of Ernie's ashes igniting the huge mound of McDonald's wrappers on his desk and thereby burning down the entire city. Ben was barely managing to keep a straight face by standing apart from the others and pretending to examine the shelves of law books that had probably been bought by the yard to impress people.

"Look," said Ernie, trying unsuccessfully to seem serious. "I represent some of the biggest operators in Boston. They'll be happy to let you have an X-rated video for your own use."

"Really, Mr. McNerney," said Franklin, with just the slightest touch of indignation. "We're not interested in seeing one of those ... uh, films. We simply want one made that we would own."

"You help those smut peddlers keep their dirty

money," Margaret chimed in, shaking her finger at Ernie as if he were a rotten little boy. "Why can't you give us the same kind of help?"

From the depths of his pudgy belly, another burst of laughter exploded through Ernie.

"And you want this film so you can raise money to ban it?"

"We simply oppose lewd and lascivious displays in public," said Franklin, trying to remain polite at all cost. "The fact is, the only way we can raise enough money to present our viewpoint in the, uh, spirit of, uh, robust and open debate is to, uh, sponsor one of these films ourselves."

"Well said," Ben added, finally able to control his amusement.

He came over to sit with his colleagues in front of Ernie's desk.

"What a load of crap!" was Ernie's comment, which sent Margaret to her feet.

"Well, I never ..."

"Margaret, sit down!" Ben commanded.

Flustered, Margaret obeyed. Ben turned to Ernie.

"Just couldn't fool you, huh?"

"I never believed you were on the level for a minute," Ernie replied.

He stubbed his cigar out on the Big Mac wrappers, to Margaret's horror.

"All right, Ernie," Ben continued. "The truth is this. We've been watching these creeps make easy money for years, so we decided the hell with Decency and Morality Now! It's our turn!"

Margaret forced herself to take her eyes off the smoldering burger wrappers to stare at Ben. As she opened her mouth to protest, Ben nudged Franklin.

"Oh, yes, that's right," said Franklin, catching on. "Of course, some of the money is going back to the D.A.M.N.! organization."

The use of the acronym he, himself, cleverly snuck by them always set off Ernie's belly laugh.

"All right. I give up!" said Ernie, raising his hands in submission. "I don't believe you for a moment, but I'll help you. I don't care what your reason is. My wife would never forgive me if I let her baby brother get torn apart in that jungle. Naturally, I will expect fifteen percent of the gross."

Margaret started to object, but Ben cut her off.

"I think that's agreeable, don't you?" he asked, turning to Franklin.

"I'd say that's a mighty generous offer, Mr. McNerney," replied Franklin.

"Generous?" said Margaret, totally out of sorts by now. "That's one way of putting it!"

"Mrs. O'Leary," Ernie said gently. "I simply want to cover my expenses and make a reasonable profit. As my Contracts professor in law school, rest his soul, used to say, 'Lawyers have to eat, too.' Besides, I wouldn't miss this for the world!"

From the outer office came a bloodcurdling, "EHNIE!"

Ernie uncovered the phone from the rubble on his desk and pushed the intercom button.

"Jeanette, use the intercom!"

He smiled a weak apology to his clients. Back over the intercom came Jeanette's, "Ehnie ..."

"What is it, Jeanette?" asked Ernie, holding down the button again.

"It's almost four o'clock. Do you want me to interrupt you with that important phone call now?"

Ernie, for once, looked chagrined.

It didn't take Ernie long to get the film "in development." The first step was arranging to use the offices of the Carlton Brothers for the afternoon two days later. Al and Peep Carlton were the biggest producers of porno films in town, and they both owed Ernie. He had helped Al beat the rap on *Student Nurses at Night*. The jury had asked for three screenings before voting for acquittal. Al was so grateful he set up a scholarship fund at Ernie's law school.

As for Peep, well, there was that business with Jeanette. It was quick thinking on Ernie's part to call her his receptionist. Peep's wife may not have bought the story entirely, but she could see for herself that Jeanette was sitting there in Ernie's office every day. Peep's marriage was saved, for the moment, anyway, and Ernie gained a receptionist, of a sort.

The Carltons had put out the word in the proper circles, and a number of directors had expressed interest in doing the film. They were all cheap, fast, and turned out movies that didn't look it. Ernie was to do the interviewing here in the Carlton office and pick a director before the day was out.

The office on Commonwealth Avenue in Brighton was much plusher than Ernie's, but the thick carpet, large red velour couch, glass coffee table and wet bar spoke of money rather than taste. Posters from the Carlton Brothers' biggest sex films adorned the walls, from the sleazy exploitation of *College Sex Kittens at Play*, to the pseudo-documentary aura of *Nudity Through the Ages*.

Ernie was settling himself comfortably on the couch and lighting his cigar when Ben came in, sporting a Van Dyke beard, mirrored sunglasses, shirt open to the navel and three pounds of junk jewelry.

"What the hell ..."

Ernie took the cigar out of his mouth as he finally recognized Ben under the disguise. Ben, however, was caught up in the movie posters.

"Your clients actually make these films?" he asked, staring at a poster advertising *Star Hookers*, a film that was apparently shown in 3D. "How can they stand to look at themselves in the morning?"

"And YOU should talk? What the hell is that get-up for, anyway?"

"I thought it would help them relate to me. Besides, I don't want to be recognized."

"I don't even know why you're here in the first place."

"I want to have a say in who's going to make this movie. I don't want to risk our money on just anyone."

"Well, keep quiet and let me do the talking, okay?"

A sexy, efficient-looking woman knocked on the door, then stuck her head in.

"Mr. McNerney? Mr. Stevens is here. Shall I show him in?"

"Please do."

As the door closed again, Ben fixed himself a drink from the bar.

"I'll speak to them, and you let me know which one you like," said Ernie. "THEN you leave the filming to me, understand?"

"Sure, Ernie, just like we agreed."

Ben sat down on the couch near Ernie as the door opened again to admit Mr. Stevens, a tall, skinny man wearing a Van Dyke beard, mirrored sunglasses, shirt open to the navel and three pounds of junk jewelry.

Before Ernie could say a word, Ben leaned over and whispered in his ear, "I don't like his looks!"

Several more candidates were ushered in over the course of the afternoon. None of them were to Ben's liking. By this time, Ernie had removed his jacket and was beginning to regret letting Ben stay for the interviews.

The second-to-last director was Stu Kingsley, who looked like an alcoholic English professor. Ben and

Ernie sat glassy-eyed as Kingsley delivered a lecture on his philosophy of porno moviemaking.

"... and I find that if you give them a good story, the sex will come naturally. When I did my all-nude version of *Pygmalion,* I brought Shaw to a brand-new audience."

Ernie finally seized the moment when Kingsley paused for a quick breath.

"Thank you for your time, Mr. Kingsley," said Ernie, getting to his feet. "We'll let you know if we can work something out."

Kingsley took the cue, with the air of one who had given a successful pitch.

"Good day, then, Mr. McNerney," he said pompously as he shook Ernie's hand.

"You, too, Killer," he added, waving to Ben.

"Well?" asked Ernie, once Kingsley was gone.

"He's as bad as the rest," answered Ben. "They're all disgusting."

"We have to pick one of them."

"Don't tell me he was the last one!"

"No. There's one left. J. Taylor. He's got a few credits, but I know him only by name. I think he's kinda young."

"He can't be any worse than Professor Dipso there," said Ben, "so let's call him in."

J. Taylor was not what either man expected to see. They were not prepared for an attractive young woman to walk through the door.

"Who are you?" Ben asked, with no tact whatsoever.

"J. Taylor. Joanne Taylor, actually. I understand you're making a movie and I'd like to direct it."

Ernie shook her hand, and mustering all the charm he could find, ushered her to a chair in front of them.

"Can you work cheaply?" he asked, when everyone was settled again. "My partner and I can't offer much of a budget."

"I've been making movies at Boston University for three years," Joanne answered with total confidence. "You want cheap? You'll get cheap. Just give me the camera."

"So you're a film student?" asked Ernie, trying to show a fatherly interest in her. "What have you done professionally?"

"You ever see *Plumber's Helper*?" she asked.

"YOU did that?" Ernie was clearly impressed.

"Is it good?" Ben whispered to Ernie.

"Good?" Ernie whispered back. "I defended the owner of the theater that showed it. I had to appeal to the Supreme Judicial Court to get him off."

Ben turned back to Joanne.

"Tell me, Ms. Taylor. Why are you making dirty, I mean, adult films?"

"I want to direct," said Joanne in a tone that said she had been through this line of questioning a hundred times before, "and it's not easy for a woman to break into the business. I take any assignment I can get. Besides, the performers like working for me. They know I'm not going to abuse them. There are some real animals out there, you know!"

"Tell me about it!" laughed Ben.

"Can you work fast?" asked Ernie.

"I turned out *Coffee Break Quickie* in ten days."

Ernie nodded to Ben. "These are good credentials."

"I think my partner and I are in agreement," said Ben, trying not to sound too excited. "I'll let him make the arrangements with you."

He got up. Joanne and Ernie did the same.

"I've enjoyed meeting you, Ms. Taylor," said Ben sincerely, shaking her hand. "The pleasure was all mine."

"Wait till you see the movie," she said, giving him a rather disdainful once-over.

Chapter 5

Ben felt very much the movie mogul as he parted with Ernie and headed for the men's room to ditch his disguise. He liked this movie business, he thought, particularly when it could include good-looking women directors.

It hurt when he pulled the beard off, but he was recalling Joanne's long curly brown hair and tight jeans, so he didn't care. No question, he thought to himself, she definitely was the perfect choice to direct the film.

Of course, now they needed the perfect film for her to direct. Ernie had promised to send some scripts over to the D.A.M.N.! office by the end of the day so they could choose one. *Now, there's an interesting picture*, Ben thought. *Margaret and Franklin reading porno scripts!* He laughed to himself as he removed the jewelry and stuffed it into his backpack along with the beard and sunglasses. He buttoned his shirt to a more respectable height and headed for the Green Line.

"It should be rather exciting," said Franklin, as Ben and Margaret moved the newspapers from the office table a short time later. "Whose written words will be transformed into film? Which set of typewritten pages will form the blueprint for ..."

He was interrupted by a loud banging on the door.

"They're here!" said Ben, as he rushed over to open the door.

True enough, a messenger handed him a large manilla envelope and a clipboard with an X indicating where he was to sign for the package. Ben signed, gave the messenger a tip and closed the door.

"Better lock it," said Franklin. "It wouldn't do to have anyone walk in on us."

Ben threw the deadbolt and brought the envelope over to Franklin.

"It's rather a small package," Franklin said, turning it over in his hands. "I thought he was sending several scripts. This can't be more than one."

Franklin carefully removed the tape that was holding the package closed. He reached in and pulled out two dozen file folders of different colors. They could easily have been mistaken for high school term papers.

"These are the scripts?" Ben said, bewildered, as he picked up one of the folders.

Margaret picked up a blue one and looked inside.

"They're only a few pages each!" she exclaimed.

"It's a dirty movie, Margaret," Franklin reminded her. "They're not going to be doing much talking."

"They have to say something to each other, don't they?"

"Maybe they improvise on the set," Ben suggested. "At least this way we should be through reading them in time for my class tonight."

Margaret read the title in front of her: *"Bertha and Her Barnyard Pals."*

She read a few lines silently and threw the folder down in disgust as if the very paper were infected.

"I won't read this!" she exclaimed. "It's revolting!"

"Diary of an Alien Bondage Queen," Franklin read his title out loud. "This is rather disgusting," he said in an academic manner as he elevated his chin for a better view through his bifocals.

Another knock at the door startled them, and they all looked up from their reading.

"Hello, is anyone in?" came a feminine voice from the other side as the locked door was rattled without mercy.

"Good Lord!" exclaimed Franklin. "It's Mother. Quick! Get these out of here!"

He began stacking the folders, and the others followed suit.

"Hello, hello?!"

If the door had been a person its brain cells would have flown out its ears by now from the shaking it was getting. Franklin mercifully hurried to unlock it and admit his mother into the room.

Mrs. Abbott was definitely not a woman to contend with. She belonged to that formidable set of Beacon Hill society matrons born to wealth in Louisburg Square. Now in her late seventies, she still carried herself with the elegance of one who knew her place at the top of the world. Yet she was not without warmth and even humor, as long as she didn't have to be the one playing straight man.

"What's going on here? Why was the door locked?" she asked, directing her questions to Franklin as if he were a child of ten rather than fifty.

"Nothing, Mrs. Abbott," Ben blurted out.

Realizing he was holding the script folders, he shoved them into his backpack along with the envelope and added, "I was just showing them a project for my marketing class at BU. I was supposed to develop a campaign for colored folders."

"Ben," said Franklin, thinking quickly from long years of practice living with Mrs. Abbott. "I think any color would be nice. My thought on the matter is that an individual could simply pick any one at random and your project would have the same result."

"What is this project ...?" asked Mrs. Abbott, who couldn't let anything cross her path without knowing all the particulars.

"My thought, too," said Ben, cutting her off quickly. "In fact, I have a class tonight, so I'll just write this conclusion up on the way. Nice to see you, Mrs. Abbott."

Before she could respond, Ben grabbed his backpack and was out the door.

"You know, Franklin," said Mrs. Abbott as the door slammed shut. "Young Benjamin has a real head on his shoulders. You watch him. He'll go far."

Ben was glad that Ernie's office was not far away. It was on Chauncy Street, not far from Tremont, so he could drop the folders off and catch the Green Line at the Boylston Station. If he didn't have to wait long for a train, he might have a chance of making it to his class on time.

Jeanette was behind the receptionist desk when Ben rushed in. She appeared to be doing some actual work in the form of two-finger typing from a Dictaphone machine. Ben set his backpack down on a corner of her desk, pulled the colored folders out, and fanned them out in front of her.

"Pick a color, any color, Jeanette," Ben said.

"Wha ...?" She took off the headset, which Ben could now see was connected to a Walkman.

"Come on, Jeanette. Just pick one. I have a class."

"Whatevah," she said, taking a red folder from the middle of the fan.

Ben took the folder from her hand and put it on the desk. He grabbed the envelope from his backpack and put the other folders in it. Then he put the envelope in front of her on the desk and the red folder back in her hand.

"Tell Ernie we decided on this script, OK?"

"Shu-ah. Whatevah," Jeanette replied, putting her headphones back on her ears without bothering to look at Ben.

"Thanks, Jeanette," said Ben, as he rushed out of the office and back to the elevators.

When he was gone, Jeanette, swaying to the rhythm

on her Walkman, opened the folder containing the script for *Adam and Eve and Rhonda and Joey.* She read the first page.

"Hey, Ehnie! They got a wicked good script he-ah," she yelled, and continued to read.

Chapter 6

The rush-hour crush had peaked by the time Ben descended into the Boylston Street T Station, yet the outbound Green Line was still crowded enough that he had to stand. He didn't mind. The advantage of sitting was that he could read. But standing, his arm looped around a pole, he was more in tune with the train as it rolled and pitched along under the Back Bay.

Even after ten years in Boston, he still got a kick out of the subway. As he read the ads on the walls – promising he could learn conversational Urdu in six weeks and offering to improve his bustline – he felt on top of the world, rather than under it.

Ben never regretted leaving St. Louis. It wasn't that he disliked his hometown, or that he didn't miss his family. Had he stayed, he might have been settled into a real career by now. Perhaps he would even be married and living in the suburbs, he thought, with a certain bemused horror.

But Boston felt like Someplace. Maybe it was because the city was perched on the edge of the United States, almost as far east as you could go, rather than in the middle of the country, like St. Louis, with all roads beckoning out and away.

Ben had come originally for education, transferring his junior year from a community college in St. Louis. His sister, Marlene, thirteen years his senior, had gone to nursing school in Boston. She had sent Ben a catalogue for the work-study program for business majors at Northeastern University. He applied on a whim, mostly to please his sister. To his surprise, he was accepted.

Ernie had been an idealistic young law student then, just finishing his second year. Marlene met him at the Head-of-the-Charles crew regatta when they were both trying to find their respective school teams and party areas along the river bank. They realized neither one of them would even know what they were looking for once they found it, so they spent the afternoon with each other instead, laughing and joking and having a great time. They were married a year later when Ernie graduated.

Today, Marlene had her own successful career as a nurse-practitioner while raising three boys. She still found Ernie funny and enjoyed his company. What she thought of the direction Ernie's career had taken Ben never asked.

After graduation, Ben held a series of supposedly career-path jobs in the big Boston insurance firms. The paths, however, all turned out to be dead-ends. He also tried stock brokerage along the way, but didn't have the stomach for losing other people's money. Frustrated, he finally took the job as a shift manager for the 7-Eleven below his apartment on Charles Street at the foot of

Beacon Hill and enrolled in an MBA program at Boston University.

What he would do with an MBA Ben wasn't quite sure, but he thought it might at least expand his options. When Franklin Abbott offered him the job as Executive Director of Decency and Morality Now! Ben didn't even have to think about it. He had worked at the 7-Eleven for two years, and had completed more than a year's worth of classes for his two-year MBA program.

Scheduling his classes around his shifts at the 7-Eleven had sometimes been difficult. Ben's new employers promised him the flexibility he needed to take the rest of his second-year classes whenever they fell during the day or evening. That the organization was not exactly mainstream didn't matter to him, either. Franklin Abbott was a member of a prominent family, and working for him might help Ben gain entree into the tight-knit Boston business circle.

Ben genuinely liked Franklin. Though not a regular customer by any means, Franklin occasionally stopped in for a newspaper or coffee in the morning, or after seeing a play at the nearby Lyric Stage Theatre, of which he was a patron. When the store was not busy, particularly when Ben was on the night shift, they would sometimes have lively conversations about the arts in Boston or some other topic of interest to both of them.

It wasn't hard for Ben to find an opportunity to mention that he was working his way through an MBA program at Boston University. Franklin was impressed, and asked Ben if he knew how to file the paperwork to incorporate his new organization as a non-profit. He was willing to pay, he said, but his personal lawyer would charge an exorbitant fee to do it.

Ben quickly offered to talk to his brother-in-law, whom he hoped he could cajole into doing it for almost nothing. When Ernie realized the antipornography organization had yet to be named, and that he could choose one himself if he filed the paperwork, he offered his services for free. The choice of name slipped by Franklin and Margaret, who both failed to see the acronym until the papers were signed, sealed and delivered to the government.

D.A.M.N.! had not been able to keep an Executive Director for long. The organization had been too small to hire someone with good credentials, and too sensitive in nature for others. Franklin was also not about to advertise the position for fear of attracting crackpots. Thus when D.A.M.N.! was in the market for a new Executive Director, Ben was a prime candidate. By all accounts, it was a good move, and Ben's part in the naming of the organization by suggesting Ernie had long been forgotten.

The outbound local Green Line jammed more people into its belly at the Arlington, Copley and Auditorium stations before losing any appreciable numbers at

Kenmore. Then it began heading up out of the tunnel toward the BU stops.

Ben was already late when he reached his classroom, but there was a note on the door stating that the class was cancelled for the day. By way of saving face for the professor, the students were admonished to use the time to work on their semester projects.

Relieved, Ben headed back along Commonwealth Avenue toward Kenmore Square and turned into The Library, a cafeteria-style student hangout. He bought a sandwich, coffee and brownie, then found a table in the back corner.

The decor of the restaurant was true to its name. Long tables extended out on either side of open metal stacks filled with volumes of indistinct character. These were obviously from library discards, as most of the books still carried their old Dewey Decimal numbers.

Ben spread his books and notebooks out on the table and began to study. He was quickly immersed in his work. From where he was sitting, he couldn't see the dramatic entrance of an attractive woman and three young men, all carrying pieces of film equipment, and all dripping wet. The quartet chose a table on the other side of the book stacks from Ben. The youngest man in the group, Jake, hurried off to buy the coffee as the others stacked their equipment in a pile behind the table.

"Did you catch the look on that guy's face when the sprinkler went off?" asked Larry, one of the remaining young men, laughing, as he settled into his chair.

"At least he knows the thing works," offered his friend Marty.

"I loved the firemen when they saw the camera," said the young woman, "all dressed up in their slickers with those boots and hats, waving their axes for all they were worth!"

"Hi MOM!" said Larry, doing a fireman-before-the-camera imitation.

"It looked like Halloween!" said Marty.

"We should have some great footage – if any of it comes out," said the woman.

"I think we got that coat over the camera in time," Larry said. "At least it didn't look wet."

Jake returned with a tray of coffees, cream and sugar packets, and a plate of brownies.

"I'm really sorry, guys," he said earnestly, passing the coffees around. "How was I to know that thing would go off!"

"It's okay, Jake," said the woman, with a noticeable tone of amused sarcasm. "It takes real talent to put a 1000-watt studio light under a heat detector."

"I didn't think about looking up at the ceiling, too," poor Jake responded. "I was having enough trouble with the lighting as it was."

"Don't worry about it," replied the woman. "After all, it wasn't MY landlord we were interviewing."

"Oh, my God!" said Jake, a thought just now sinking in. "It was MY landlord!"

At this point, the other three at the table laughed so

loud that Ben, on the other side of the bookcase, looked up from his work.

"I still think we missed a good bet," said Larry to the attractive young woman. "We should have taken off all our clothes and done your new porno flick right there."

Ben put down his pen.

"Of course, someone might wonder why we were staging an orgy in the midst of an indoor thunderstorm," Marty added.

"We could have brought in a cow and called it *Noah's Ark*," said Larry, obviously now on a roll.

"I've got some great ideas for casting the jackasses," answered the woman. "Let's have a little respect for your director. After all, you're in the presence of genius, my good men."

As the laughter escalated, Ben wanted to see the quartet on the other side of the shelf. He took a book out from his side, then tried to pull one from the opposite side to create a peephole so he could see through to the other table. However, the book went crashing through the wrong way.

Larry was sitting closest to the shelf and picked up the book. He intended to put it back in place, but instead shoved it all the way through onto Ben's table. Ben attempted to slide it gently and quietly back into place without calling attention to himself. Larry seized the moment and pushed the book back to Ben's side. Ben again tried to sneak the book back into place, but Larry held it so Ben couldn't push it in, while Marty shoved another book onto Ben's table.

Ben escalated the battle by sending four books through, and the others counterattacked with about a dozen from their side. When the manager realized that a holy book war was taking place within his borders, he commanded the warriors to clean up and take their leave, thank you very much.

The young woman, meanwhile, curious to meet such a worthy opponent, ventured around the stacks into enemy territory. She found Ben on the floor, laughing, covered in books.

"Are you all right?" asked the young woman.

Ben's suspicions were now confirmed, and he smiled as he looked into the beautiful face of Joanne Taylor, movie director.

"My friends warned me about becoming buried in my books!"

The Esplanade that runs along the Charles River in Boston is probably one of the few urban parks in the country that is still safe for a young man and woman to walk at night. It may be because of the narrow width and lack of cover for criminal wannabes, or simply the sheer numbers of healthy young joggers, dog walkers and students who clearly make unlikely candidates for assault victims.

Ben and Joanne took the footbridge across Storrow Drive at Bay State Road and strolled along the water's edge toward the Harvard Bridge. Joanne wasn't quite sure why she accepted his offer to walk her home. He was cute, she thought, and he obviously had a sense of humor. But there was something vaguely familiar about him, and she was curious to figure out what it was.

"Are you SURE we haven't met before?" she asked as they passed by the outdoor workout center.

"I don't think so. Maybe you've just seen me at The Library. I go there a lot."

Ben was uncomfortable with this line of conversation and changed the subject.

"So, you're a film student. What were you filming?

"A cinema vérité-type thing: *A Day in the Life of a Boston Landlord.*"

"Really? Were you shooting the arson sequence tonight?"

"No, but that's a great idea for a plot point!" Joanne answered, laughing. "Actually, we had a slight problem with a bright light and a dim techie. If we ever finish this, I'll use it as my Masters project."

"So you're a graduate student?" Ben asked.

"Maybe a perpetual one. I'm thinking of hanging around for my Doctorate."

"Don't you want to go out and make real movies?"

"Of course I do," said Joanne. "But it's still not easy for women to break in as directors. Even in the business of illusions, you have to be a realist once in a while."

Now it was her turn to change the subject.

"So, what worthy and stimulating discipline are you pursuing in these hallowed halls?"

"Business Administration."

"Speaking of realism, eh?" said Joanne. "Are you taking a leave of absence from the corporate jungle for the ol' MBA?"

"Actually, they haven't let me in that world yet," answered Ben, "unless you count managing the Beacon Hill 7-Eleven, which is more like the corporate suburbs. That's why I'm back in school. I realized I was never going to get anywhere without it."

"And where do you want to get with it?" asked Joanne, with real interest.

Ben shook his head. "I don't know. Just somewhere else, I guess."

He stopped walking and turned to look at her.

"I don't know why I'm telling you this."

"I guess because we have so much in common," said Joanne gently.

"We do?"

"Sure. We're both on the outside looking in right now."

They started walking again in silence. Suddenly, Ben gave a sigh of relief.

"You know," he said. "You're really a lot different than I thought you would be."

"Huh?" said Joanne, somewhat taken aback. "So you do know me, then?"

"No, no," said Ben, thinking fast. "I mean from when you were with your friends in The Library."

"Oh, yeah. Well, I have my insecurities, just like everyone else."

"I didn't mean that. I, ah ... I mean you're really nice. You seem like a sensitive person."

"I'd better get going," she said, picking up her pace, uncomfortable with this turn in the conversation. "I'm starting to get chilly."

"And I have to go to work early tomorrow morning," said Ben, looking at his watch to cover the awkwardness of the moment.

"At the 7-Eleven?" asked Joanne, relieved to be back on solid, factual conversational ground.

"No," said Ben. "Actually, I'm an office manager for a small public service, non-profit organization downtown."

"A charity?"

"Something like that. How about you?"

"I do an occasional independent film – when I get an offer. It's good experience and it gets me by financially."

They climbed the stairs to the Harvard Bridge and walked toward Beacon Street.

"This is where I live," said Joanne, stopping in front of a tall building on the corner of Massachusetts Avenue and Beacon Street. "It's been really nice talking with you."

"The pleasure was all mine," said Ben, looking straight into her beautiful eyes.

Something deep within Joanne stirred at his phrase.

"Are you sure we haven't met before?"

Chapter 7

The arrangements for shooting took Ernie and Joanne a week, from casting through lining up locations and equipment. The actual filming took another twelve days, and editing a week more. The film came in under budget. The funding came from Franklin through Ernie's office, to keep the bookkeeping off the D.A.M.N.! ledgers. Joanne was too busy with the film to think much about the mystery man from The Library, and Ben knew he had to stay away from her or risk blowing his cover.

By June, the film was ready for theatrical release, just in time for the tourist season. Ernie booked the small screening room in the Carlton Brothers office so his clients could view the finished product. Not wanting any witnesses to their arrival, Franklin drove Margaret and Ben to their destination instead of taking a cab. Peep Carlton had thoughtfully offered his private parking place behind the building so Franklin wouldn't have to search for a place on the street.

Margaret looked more than slightly suspicious in a huge trench coat, dark glasses and a beige scarf tied over her hair so that her face was almost totally concealed. Ernie had propped the back door open with the latest issue of *Penthouse* borrowed from the Carlton Brothers reception room. Ben held the door open and picked up the magazine. With a last check down the alley to be sure they weren't spotted, the trio ducked into the building.

Ernie was alone in the screening room when the D.A.M.N.! contingent entered. He greeted them warmly, shaking Franklin's hand with enthusiasm.

"We did it!" he said proudly. "We brought the picture in under budget, and a more X-rated film I wouldn't want to see. I sure hope this is what you wanted."

"And how did our director do?" Franklin asked, trying to strike the right posture between interest and nonchalance.

Ben tried to look only casually interested in the response while handing the *Penthouse* back to Ernie. Margaret, meanwhile, was taking off her coat, dark glasses and scarf and settling herself uneasily into a seat in the middle of the room.

"She did a fantastic job," said Ernie. "When this director goes Hollywood, it'll be the porno industry's loss."

"These days, who can tell the difference," said Margaret as she grabbed the armrests and braced herself for the distasteful viewing ahead.

"Well, I suppose we should see the film," said Franklin, walking over to sit one seat away from Margaret. "It's not likely to be a pleasant experience, but if we're going to protest this film in a big way, we have to know what kind of garbage is in it."

"It's a dirty job, but somebody's got to do it," said Ben with a grin, taking a seat in the row behind the others.

"You know, that's just what I tell people about MY job," said Ernie.

He sat down next to Margaret and patted her hand, which was clutching the armrest in fearful anticipation.

Margaret lurched her hand away from him.

"And well you should! Of all the disgusting ..."

"Margaret," said Franklin, sotto voce, "Mr. McNerney has been very helpful to us. I don't think we should antagonize him."

"It's all right, Franklin, I'm used to it," said Ernie in an overloud whisper, leaning across Margaret.

With a laugh, he turned his head toward the hidden projection booth in the rear.

"Ready when you are."

The lights dimmed and the credits for *Adam and Eve and Rhonda and Joey* began to roll, accompanied by tinny 1940s-style big-band music. The credits were brief and ended with "Directed by J. Taylor," as the camera dollied up to the front door of a suburban tract home.

The scene then cut to the inside, where a buxom young woman in a flimsy peignoir was dusting with a feather duster. Someone knocked on the door. The woman opened it to reveal the milkman. She let him in. As she started to remove his clothes, the doorbell rang. The woman of the house left the milkman and opened the door to admit another, slightly older woman in a brief halter top and shorts holding a measuring cup.

"I've come to borrow a cup of sugar," she said.

The first woman stepped aside to let her in, followed by

the postman, who had just come up the walk. The woman in the peignoir returned to the milkman as the doorbell rang again. This time it was a meter reader and a grocery delivery boy. They were both admitted as the phone rang.

Depending on one's point of view, it was either all downhill or all uphill from there. The movie was everything Margaret could have imagined in a porno film, and more, but done with tongue firmly in cheek, a tone decidedly lost on her.

"I didn't know fourteen people could DO that together," she said at one point, totally bewildered.

At the end of the movie, the young woman of the house was standing in the doorway, back to the audience, waving goodbye to her guests with her feather duster. She didn't have a stitch on.

"Bye, come again," she said.

The camera moved in for a close-up of the words, "THE END," superimposed over her bum.

The lights came up in the screening room, catching Ernie laughing, Ben smirking but trying to cover it up, Franklin looking like he couldn't make up his mind whether to be amused or appalled, and Margaret simply stunned.

"'The End.' That was too much!" laughed Ernie, tears in his eyes.

Margaret just stared straight ahead and muttered to herself, "I can't believe it, I can't believe it!"

"I think Margaret needs some fresh air," said Franklin, rising to his feet.

He lifted her gently by the arm as she continued to mutter to herself.

"Come along, Margaret," he said, then turned to Ben, "Bring her things. We'll wait for you out back."

Ben reached over the seat and started gathering the pieces of Margaret's disguise.

"So, Ben, is that what you wanted?" asked Ernie once Franklin and Margaret had cleared the room.

"I'm not sure," answered Ben. "My eyeballs are still steamed up."

"Peep Carlton has agreed to a one-week run at his BeauX Arts Cinema next month. I've made you into a pornographer, Ben. Marlene would kill me if she knew. I just hope you know what you're doing."

"Don't worry about us," said Ben. "We can handle it.

"I hope so, kid," said Ernie seriously.

"See ya," said Ben, turning to go. At the door, he turned back to Ernie.

"Ernie ..."

"Yeah, kid?"

"Thanks."

Ernie just waved as if to say, "No biggie." Ben took the cue and went out to find Margaret and Franklin in the back alley. Ernie sat down again. As he thought about the film, he started laughing again. He turned to the projection booth.

"You wanna run that again?"

Chapter 8

Even in the latter decades of the twentieth century, the nineteenth still shrouded Louisburg Square – the most exclusive address on Boston's Beacon Hill. The brick row houses facing the wrought-iron enclosed garden had seen the most prominent Bostonians come and go for nearly two hundred years. Louisa May Alcott died on the square. Of all the addresses in the city, Louisburg Square was still the one of choice for old money and new, Brahmins as well as olive oil importers.

The Abbott fortune was definitely old money, the source being generally noted as "real estate and investments." That the "real estate" happened to include most of the old Scollay Square burlesque district was not mentioned, either by the Abbotts or anyone else of good breeding. The former center of sin and deprivation had now become respectable, in a manner of speaking, as the site of the new City Hall and other offices of Government Center.

The "Investments" were assumed to fall under the category of "financial," and it certainly would have been in bad taste to have inquired further of the Abbotts. Even Franklin's own mother was oblivious to the true origins of her husband's money. Her own family had been in shipping, a lofty enough vocation, unless one considered the Boston origins in the triangle trade – slaves, cotton, molasses and booze – which it would have been beneath Mrs. Abbott to do.

In fact, when Mrs. Abbott looked in her closets, she saw only her gowns for the charity balls she would so often chair, her Chanel suits, and the other badges of her station. She certainly did not see the family skeletons lurking in the shadows.

But Franklin did. He saw them all – the tattoo artists in their seedy parlors, the burlesque dancers with wan faces and desperate eyes, the women of the streets, the sailors wasting their wages on sin. They had all poured money in one way or another into the landlord's pocket. That landlord was named Justin Abbott, Franklin's great-grandfather, who was succeeded by his son, Nathan, Franklin's grandfather.

By the time of Franklin's father, Joseph Abbott, Scollay Square was already being supplanted as the city's sin district by what was known as the Combat Zone. This was a raunchy neighborhood of peep shows and "adult" cinemas bordered by the downtown shopping district on one side, and the Common, the Theatre District and Chinatown on the others. By then, however, it didn't matter to the Abbott fortune. Having sold their property to the city for a handsome sum, the Abbotts no longer collected rents via the wages of sin.

Joseph went to Harvard and married the heiress to the Mayflower Shipping Line. He dabbled in politics, and had a perfectly respectable career managing his own family investments before dying of a heart attack during a particularly worrisome bridge game at the Harvard Club at the age of sixty-three.

Franklin, for want of anything else to do, had followed in his father's footsteps – Harvard degree in finance, a dabble in politics, and managing the family investment portfolio. He had been in love once, passionately in love with a pretty young poetry student in his Harvard days. They had planned to wed, but Mrs. Abbott didn't approve as the girl was from Kansas City.

Caught between his love and his mother, Franklin dragged his heels until the young woman finally gave up, joined the Peace Corps and was posted to Fiji. There she met an aspiring artist, whom she later married. The last Franklin heard of her, she and her artist were poor but happy living in a condo they were able to purchase in the Marina District of San Francisco.

Franklin was only thirty-two when his father died and his mother required his full attention. Mother and son toured Europe together until their grief was healed. They came home and settled into a comfortable and non-threatening life in the Louisburg Square mansion.

It was while tidying up his father's affairs that Franklin stumbled on the truth of his family. The venerable library and office in the house had been his father's sanctuary. Now it was Franklin's. While his father was alive, Franklin would not have considered inspecting anything in it, particularly the old leather-bound ledgers that lined the back wall. Now it was his duty to do so, in order to properly evaluate the estate in his new role of heir and manager.

The ledgers for his father's tenure were straight-forward accounts of stocks, bonds and mutual funds, with dates of purchase and sale, amounts of interest and other facts carefully noted. The older ledgers, however, revealed a different story. These listed real estate holdings, including tenants. Most would not have raised the eyebrows of anyone at the Boston Atheneum. But included in the lists were Ivan's Body Art, Charlie's Tattoos, Rosie's Goodtime Palace, Sailors Heaven, and many others simply noted with a name or letters.

A day's research at the Boston Public Library, including a few hours with the Library's photo archivist, filled in the picture for Franklin. His family had made their wealth on the debauchery of others in the city he so dearly loved.

Franklin went home that night and announced to his mother that he was going away for the weekend. Before she could protest, he had packed a small bag and walked out of the house. He needed to get away from the Square, from all the trappings of wealth and his decadent fortune. He checked into the Harvard Club, and then spent three days wandering the city.

He actually found his way on the T down to Government Center. He walked the entire district, from State Street and down Cambridge Street as far over as the North End. He tried to conjure up in his mind how it was then – the burlesque houses, the cheap restaurants and cheaper hotels, the tattoo parlors and women of the night.

But the austere brick plaza surrounding City Hall held few echoes of former days. The JFK government building, the crescent of Center Plaza hiding the lovely old courthouse from view, the ugly parking structure behind the police station and the broadcasting buildings – nothing offered hints of what had once been. They did, however, attest to someone's having made a fortune on the sale of the land to the government. That someone, of course, was Joseph Abbott.

It was when he walked back uptown and took a shortcut over to the Boylston T Station that Franklin found a way to atone for what he perceived as his family's disgrace. He had never been in the Combat Zone before. Stumbling upon it, he felt like he had fallen into some sort of perverse Disneyland.

"Girls, Girls, Girls," "Adult XXX," the signs screamed at him. On every corner, he was offered women. In another frame of mind, Franklin would have run for his life, back to the shelter of the Square and Mother. But today, he walked the whole district, drinking it in, trying to let his senses comprehend the sin that was being lived and offered for a price.

Finally, as he headed out of the Combat Zone, he passed the adult movie houses, with the BeauX Arts Cinema the most prominent. A poster to the side of the theater's ticket booth advertised a particularly repulsive-sounding film.

Across it was a banner stating, "Banned in Boston." At that moment, Franklin knew he had found his direction. He would become a crusader for decency and morality in his city. He would use some of his family money to fight the very evil on which that fortune had been made.

In the years between Franklin's epiphany and the formation of D.A.M.N.! he had served on many a mayor's and governor's council for the cleanup of the Combat Zone. But he grew frustrated at the stalemates and inaction of the government bodies. Then one morning, while reading the *Boston Globe*, he came across a picture of some South Boston matrons picketing a particularly heinous film at the BeauX Arts. The leader's name was given as one Mrs. Margaret O'Leary. There was no real organization to the group. It was merely a result of one mother's son having been admitted, at age seventeen, to the movie, and then being overheard bragging about it.

Franklin looked up the telephone number of Mrs. O'Leary and gave her a call. The eventual collaboration culminated in D.A.M.N.! and the rest, as they say, is history.

Franklin was reading his *Wall Street Journal* in the library of his Louisburg Square mansion when Martha, the family maid and cook, brought him a fresh pot of coffee and the news that Ben and Margaret had just arrived.

"Please show them in, Martha," said Franklin,

folding his paper neatly and placing it on the antique butler's table next to his chair. He got up to greet his guests, whom he could hear talking in the hallway.

"The more I think about this, the more I don't like it," said Margaret, handing Martha her coat.

Even though the weather had turned warm, Margaret detected a threat of a drizzle in the air and had worn her lightweight yellow raincoat just in case. One could never be too prepared, according to Margaret.

"We've gone through this before," Ben pleaded. "It's a little late to turn back now."

"Something's going to go wrong, I just know it!" Margaret insisted, as she and Ben followed Martha down the hall toward the library.

"Nothing's going to go wrong, Margaret. Our plan is working according to schedule."

"Good morning Ben, Margaret," said Franklin warmly, ushering them into the room. "Won't you sit down. Would you like some coffee?"

He indicated two comfortable-looking leather chairs across from his, flanking the huge granite fireplace. As Ben and Margaret were settling themselves into their chairs, Franklin rang for Martha, who almost immediately brought in a tray with a larger, silver coffee pot, cups and saucers, and small pastries from Rebecca's.

"Now," began Franklin, once everyone was settled, coffee cup and pastry in hand. "Is something amiss in our scheme?"

"No, Franklin. In fact, everything's perfect," said Ben, before Margaret could answer. "They love us."

"Who loves us?" asked Margaret, slightly off-guard by Ben's opening.

"The reviewers. The Carlton Brothers arranged for a screening for some, uh, trade publications last month. I'm pleased to say we open in Boston tomorrow with some very strong reviews."

He opened his briefcase and took out some photocopies of newspaper and magazine articles.

"Just how important are reviews for a film of this nature?" asked Franklin.

"For your average film," said Ben, "not very much. But when you're trying to create a high-profile movie, like *Deep Throat* or *Behind the Green Door* ..."

"All right, all right," Margaret cut in. "They do their ugly little job well. Spare us the details!"

"I'm sorry," said Ben. "I was just answering Franklin's question and thought you'd like to know how thing are going. Would you like to see the reviews?"

"Certainly not!" responded Margaret.

"I AM a little curious," said Franklin, which sent a look of distain his way from Margaret. "It can't hurt to take a look."

"I figured you'd prefer not to have to look at the publications they're in, so I made copies just of the reviews."

Ben handed Franklin and Margaret each a sheaf of stapled photocopies. Franklin began to flip through his, while Margaret quickly turned hers face down on her lap.

One passage caught Franklin's eye, which actually twinkled in amusement. He adjusted his glasses on his nose and read out loud: "... a sense of playfulness and fun too often missing from the genre ..."

"Mighty fancy talk for a dirty movie, Ben."

"What makes you think the people who'll see our movie know how to read?" asked Margaret contemptuously.

"Good point, Margaret," said Ben. "And that's where you come in."

Chapter 9

Like every other big city in the country, Boston's airwaves had become saturated with the clatter of thousands of people talking. The TV networks, of course, sent in Oprah, Sally, Geraldo, Phil, Arsenio, Jay, David, Montel, Maury and even Whoopi. But Boston also had its own homegrown variety. One cable station offered twenty-four hours of talk shows on everything from arts and local politics to child-rearing and alien abduction.

The most popular of the locals was "Boston is Talking," with host Pamela Kilroy, a former consumer affairs reporter, now in her mid-thirties. Pamela had just finished a discussion with a noted Harvard professor on his startling theory that whales beach themselves on Cape Cod in response to radio waves emanating from communications satellites. The conversation stopped just short of blaming the massive doses of human talk show chatter the animals might be subjected to for their tragic impulse to commit mass suicide. Luckily for Pamela, the director signaled that it was time to thank her guest and take a station break right at the point when that conclusion might logically be reached.

Once back on the set, every hair and fiber of her

being restored to its rightful perfect location, the red lights on the cameras blinked "on" and Pamela Kilroy was again on the air.

"Our next guest is Margaret O'Leary, president of Boston-based antipornography group Decency and Morality Now! Margaret, what is the situation here in Boston at the moment on the pornography front?"

The camera moved in on Margaret's face to avoid showing her hands clutching her armrests for dear life.

"We've studied the sort of entertainment currently playing in the adult Entertainment District in Boston," she began, a bit stiffly, as if she had memorized her speech, "or, as it is more popularly known, the Combat Zone."

"And what did you find?" asked Pamela, with professional interest.

"It's like an open sewer!"

Margaret suddenly dropped her stiffness and gave herself to the soap-box moment with abandon.

"Anything having to do with sex is for sale there," she ranted. "I don't know how the leaders of the City of Boston can stand idly by while this so-called entertainment flourishes!"

"Could you give us an example?"

Pamela was the perfect journalist, bringing the conversation around to specifics.

"Well," said Margaret, with a proper indignant huff, "there's one film that just opened there this week. It's called *Adam and Eve and Rhonda and Joey.* It's nothing more than a ninety-minute marathon of perversion!"

"In your professional view," asked Pamela, "would you say that it's obscene?"

"Would I!" Margaret responded, then seized her moment and looked right into the camera. "This film makes Sodom and Gomorrah look like *The House at Pooh Corner!*"

The next day, across a poster for *Adam and Eve and Rhonda and Joey* outside the BeauX Arts Cinema, a banner was pasted that read: "A ninety-minute marathon of perversion ... Makes Sodom and Gomorrah look like *The House at Pooh Corner!*" – Margaret O'Leary, President, D.A.M.N.!

It was not quite noon, and already the banner was doing its job. Passersby had been snagged all morning by the enticing words and lured into the theater, depositing six dollars apiece at the ticket booth as they entered. The protest occurring outside didn't hurt business, either. A group of thirty or more women, led by Margaret, carried signs that read such things as: "Stamp out sin," "Scorn Porn," and "Clean up Boston."

Margaret spotted Franklin getting out of a cab, and left the group to go greet him. Taking his coat sleeve, she dragged him over to see the poster.

"Look at this," she exclaimed. "Did they have to use that abbreviation?"

"Not so loud," said Franklin, pulling her aside.

"Forget about the acronym, Margaret. They're using you to sell their movie. You're supposed to be angry about THAT!"

"But couldn't they have spelled it out?"

"They probably needed to save space," Franklin answered, not caring himself, but grasping at any straw to appease Margaret's anguish and get her mind back on the business at hand.

"But I've never seen my name in front of a theater before. I feel like Gene Shalit!"

Margaret picked up some leaflets from a small folding table behind the protesters. She handed one to a man in a business suit. The man took the offering, skimmed it, and went directly into the theater.

"It's working, Margaret," said Franklin, with a nod toward the man. "All this publicity is making this the hot film to see."

Ben had been on a coffee break when Franklin arrived. He tossed his cup on top of an already overflowing trashcan and came up to his partners in slime.

"Al Carlton just told Ernie that he wants to hold us over for another two weeks. It's happening! Come on, time to protest!"

With the air of a high school cheerleader, Ben picked up a megaphone from the protest table. Standing to the side of the group, he led them in a cheer: "Porno shows have got to close! Porno shows have got to close!"

Franklin had never been to Margaret's house before, but he thought it would be a nice gesture to drive her home after the protest. It had been a long day, and Margaret had been on her feet for most of it. Besides, he rarely drove his Mercedes, preferring to call a cab and not have to worry about finding a safe lot in which to park.

The elation of the day had put him in an adventurous mood. So, before the protest was officially over, he hailed a taxi for Louisburg Square and picked up his car. He was relieved to see that Margaret was still chatting with a few of her cohorts when he got back to the theater.

Franklin was curious to see Southie again. As a youth, he had occasionally sailed into one of the yacht clubs there. Most of his yachting days had been spent in Marblehead. It would never have occurred to him to revisit the area on his own. It wasn't the sort of thing an Abbott would do.

But now, here he was, in the middle of South Boston, looking down Broadway to Pleasure Bay. It made him realize, a bit wistfully, that he hadn't been yachting in at least ten years. He had enough friends with large yachts he could often sail on that he never bothered owning one of his own.

Margaret directed him to pull into the driveway of her house. When he had stopped and set the brake, she invited him in. Ben was to appear on a radio talk show in less than an hour. Margaret suggested they could listen to it in her living room over a nice cup of tea.

The O'Leary house was much larger than Franklin had expected. It was old, in that graceful part of Southie between Summer and Farragut that looked out on the yacht clubs and the harbor. Huge maple trees shaded the two-story house in summer, and the leaves turned to fire in the fall.

Funny, thought Franklin, *one hears about the St. Patrick's Day celebrations and the problems between the Irish and the Black students in the schools, but forgets that people also just live here, too.*

South Boston, had, in fact, been a well-heeled part of the city at one time. Now, of course, it was predominantly Irish, as could be seen by the names of the pubs and shops. French-Canadians, Poles, and other ethnic groups also shared the peninsula that jutted into Boston Harbor south of the boatyards and the wharfs.

Margaret was fourth-generation Irish on her father's side, and third on her mother's. Her paternal great-grandparents, Mary and Michael Hannaghan, had sailed from Cork during the potato famine of the 1840s. Mary had found work as a seamstress for wealthy families, possibly even the Abbotts, if it could be known. Her husband toted barges and lifted bales on the thriving Boston docks. Their children and grandchildren joined the ranks of Boston's Finest, fought the city's fires and kept the MTA running.

The O'Leary's, Margaret's husband's people, were relative newcomers, having fled Ireland after the Easter Rebellion of 1916. The pub they opened in Southie, appropriately called O'Leary's, was still a favorite watering hole. Today, well-dressed, middle-class and middle-aged Irish-Americans could be found munching pretzels and downing pints of Guinness while happily singing Kill-the-Brit songs with gusto.

Margaret was rarely one of them, even though, since her husband's passing five years ago, she was a part owner of the pub, along with his three brothers. *Why waste time and energy on problems in another country,* she thought, *when there were so many things to meddle with right here in Boston?*

Apart from D.A.M.N.!, Margaret confined her political activity to helping prepare the uniforms for the Sons and Daughters of Erin Marching Band and Drill Team in the yearly St. Patrick's Day Parade. She had seen six children and countless nieces and nephews through their marching days. Now and again, she would participate in the activities of various Irish charitable organizations, such as the Ancient Order of Hibernians.

The living room mantlepiece in Margaret's well-kept house was covered with various shapes and sizes of frames from which pictures of handsome freckle-faced children of various shapes and sizes grinned out at Franklin as he entered the room. He walked over for a closer look while Margaret tidied up a few newspapers in the room that didn't really need tidying up.

"So good of you to drive me home, Franklin."

"I'm only too happy to, Margaret."

"I hate to admit it, but I'm bushed! I haven't yelled so much in one day since my son played fullback for BC. Oh, that was a time!"

Franklin lifted his chin a little so he could see through the bottom of his bifocals and pointed to a picture of a sturdy-looking, red-haired young man in a football uniform and pose.

"Boston College, huh? Would this be the fellow?"

"My youngest boy, Michael. He played on one of the greatest teams in BC history. He's now a coach at our parish high school," Margaret said with pride. "Let me put the kettle on. I'll just be a moment."

Margaret was one of those women who has trouble sitting still for even a second, no matter how tired she is. She fussed about the kitchen while she waited for the water to boil in the teakettle, fixing a tray with cookies and her best bone china tea cups and saucers to take in.

Franklin was seated when she came back into the living room, and he rose to take the tray from her.

"Set it right here on the table," Margaret said, clearing off a candy dish in the shape of a shamrock and straightening the lace doily underneath.

Franklin set the tray down where he was told and reseated himself. Margaret poured out.

"I think this is going to be a successful venture,

Margaret," Franklin said, by way of opening a conversation.

"We do seem to be drumming up business for that disgusting movie," Margaret acknowledged, as she handed him a cup of tea on a dainty saucer.

"Just remember that every ticket sold to that abominable film is another contribution to D.A.M.N.!'s good works."

Noticing Margaret's wince at the acronym, Franklin added, "I'm sorry."

"Oh, never mind," said Margaret, with a certain tone of relieved resignation in her voice. "After producing a dirty movie, a little unintentional swearing seems like a relatively minor thing. Please, have some cream and sugar, and a cookie."

Franklin helped himself to a half-teaspoon of sugar and mixed it into his tea. He usually preferred his tea black, or with lemon, but Margaret's strong Irish brew called for sugar. The shortbread cookies were obviously store-bought, but he took one and enjoyed it.

"I hope we're doing the right thing," said Margaret, after a moment's silence while they sipped their tea. "I mean, what would Father McDonough say if he knew. I don't dare bring this to confession."

"Just think of the end result, Margaret. It's allowing us to keep our campaign going. Someday, maybe we can rid our fair city of this vice, once and for all."

"What's our next order of business, then?"

"I posted the letters to our membership this morning

while you and Ben were starting the protest. If they're as worked up as I think, our newspapers and elected officials should soon find their 'in' baskets overflowing."

Margaret was encouraged by that and ate a cookie. Suddenly, Franklin looked at his watch.

"Oh, my! We don't want to miss Ben's radio appearance."

"Mother of God!" Margaret exclaimed. "I'd almost forgotten!"

She got up and turned on a well-preserved 1938 Philco console radio that stood next to the fireplace.

"Thank goodness you remembered," said Margaret. "I try never to miss Phil Ledbetter's show, anyway. He's such a nice man. Did you know his sister's boy rides the same bus to work as my Mary Katherine?"

Chapter 10

I n the studios of "The Phil Ledbetter Show," high up in the Prudential Tower, the engineer was running some commercials prior to airtime. Phil, a young-looking forty, was sitting at the table in the studio with his guest, explaining the show's call-in system to her.

"We're on a seven-second delay, so if any of our callers should get out of hand I can cut it off before it goes out over the air."

"How about if your other guest gets out of hand?" asked the attractive young woman.

"I wouldn't worry about that. I just hope he's not going to be a no-show."

As if on cue, the engineer signaled through the control room window.

"Good," said the host. "I think that's him now."

A young female production assistant opened the door and ushered a young man over to a seat at the table. She pulled a microphone close to him and then went back out to the control room.

"Ben Porter," said Phil Ledbetter, sitting across from his two guests, "This is my other guest, Joanne Taylor. Joanne directed that X-rated movie you're here to talk about. I thought it would be interesting if she argued the other side of the issue tonight."

Ben and Joanne stared at each other, stunned. Ben was first to recover his composure.

"How do you do, Ms. Taylor," he said, offering his hand.

Mortified, Joanne limply shook it.

"I thought you said you worked for a non-profit charity," she whispered to Ben.

"I do," he whispered back. "Decency and Morality Now! has been in the red for its entire existence. YOU said you made independent films!"

"I do. My last film was made for a two-bit attorney and his sleazebag partner."

"Sleazebag?" Ben couldn't help feeling wounded at that appellation.

Phil had been listening to instructions from his engineer over his headphones, so he missed the conversation between his two guests. Their hostility he simply chalked up to a natural animosity between the opposing sides of so emotional an issue as pornography. He was thrilled. *This should be a good show tonight*, he said to himself.

The production assistant came in again and set a pitcher of water and three glasses on the table.

"We're almost set to go," said Phil, when the PA had left the room and reentered the control room.

He took his headphones off one ear and watched as the engineer signaled the seconds to airtime.

"Hello, friends," he began at the cue. "This is the Phil Ledbetter Show. My guests this evening are film director Joanne Taylor, whose latest movie is the controversial *Adam and Eve and Rhonda and Joey,* and Benjamin Porter, Executive Director of Decency and Morality Now! Good evening, Joanne and Ben. Welcome to the Phil Ledbetter Show."

"Good evening, Phil," said Ben. "The pleasure's all mine."

Joanne turned and stared at Ben. Where had she heard that phrase before, she wondered, and why did he look so dang familiar?

"Ben, your group has been particularly active in trying to shut down Ms. Taylor's film. Have you actually seen it?"

"Yes, I have, Phil. Groups such as ours are often criticized for attacking films or books without first-hand knowledge of them, so I forced myself to sit through this one."

"And how was it?" asked the genial host.

"It was the worst piece of trash ever displayed on a Boston movie screen!"

"My researchers tell me it's a very explicit film," said Phil.

"Have they seen it?" asked Ben, trying to sound indignant. "I'm sorry they had to be subjected to it on my account."

"Not to worry. They did it on their own time. Now Ms. Taylor, I was wondering ..." Phil turned to Joanne, who was still staring at Ben. "Ms. Taylor ..." Phil whispered, trying to get her attention.

"Oh, I'm sorry, yes?"

"Would you like to respond?"

"I would," said Joanne, turning to him and composing herself. "My film tries to deal with its subject honestly, rather than pretend it's something it's not. I think that's why Mr. Porter has such trouble with it."

She turned back and stared triumphantly at Ben.

"Yes, well ... let's go to the phones," said Phil, who, for once, had no idea how to respond to the guests in front of him. "The number is 617-555-6565. You're listening to the Phil Ledbetter Show, and my guests are pornographic filmmaker Joanne Taylor, and pornography fighter Benjamin Porter. And you're on the air," he said, as he pressed a button on the console in front of him.

"Hello?" said a voice from the phone lines.

"Good evening," answered Phil.

"Phil?"

"You're on the air," Phil reminded the caller.

"Oh. Hello, Phil. How're you doing?"

"I'm fine, thanks. And who is calling?"

"Oh, yes. I'm George. I'm a first-time caller, long-time listener from Jamaica Plain."

"Welcome to our show, George. Do you have a question for our guests?"

"Yes, I do. Mr. Porter?"

Ben leaned into his mike and smiled.

"I'm here."

"Were you talking about that dirty movie with all those people doing all those disgusting things with each other?" asked George.

"That's the one," Ben answered.

"Where is it playing?"

Phil cut in. "I don't think Mr. Porter wants to give this film any more publicity ..."

"I certainly don't," said Ben, loud and clear. "To think that they're showing this movie right in the heart of downtown, just a block off Boylston Street at that so-called BeauX Arts Cinema. Every day, starting at 10 a.m. Anyone with six dollars can just go in and see it!"

"Did you say 10 a.m.?" asked George.

"And every two hours after that," said Ben, only too happy to answer.

"Do you know if they check IDs?"

"George," Phil cut in, "I hate to interrupt, but we have to go to a commercial."

For another half hour, Joanne found herself in the uncomfortable position of having to defend her "art form" against the entire spectrum of antipornography viewpoints. There were calls from the religious right, the women's left, the mothers' middle, as well as from the politically and socially uptight. Her defenses were well practiced, however, and she could spiel them off with conviction, if not exactly passion. After all, she had honed them to a fare-thee-well for the last six years against her own parents.

Joanne was actually fortunate that her parents were

1960s California flower children who had dropped out and left San Jose for a commune in Vermont. Rick Taylor and Hester Crowley had Joanne in 1963, and then got married in 1967 to protest the Vietnam War. The marriage and child also just happened to earn Rick a 1Y draft status.

During the more practical 1970s, the other commune members gradually drifted away, eventually leaving the Taylor family alone on the small farm near Burlington. Rick had gained experience in the building crafts while helping to renovate the two-hundred-year-old farmhouse. He applied for and passed his contractor's exam and became a much-in-demand builder. Hester, meanwhile, finished her degree at the University of Vermont and received a teaching credential in art, in between the pregnancies and deliveries of Joanne's three brothers.

The one strong link with their urban California past for the Taylor family was the movie theater in Burlington. They saw everything that played. They were probably the first people in all of Vermont to acquire a VCR, taping every movie they could find on TV to be watched again and again. When their local country store acquired a video rental library, they thought they must have died and gone to heaven.

With hippie movie junkies for parents, it's not surprising that Joanne would catch the filmmaking bug. Her father had purchased a home movie camera at a yard sale when Joanne was young, but the family quickly tired of taking the routine videos of Joanne trying to milk the cow and her brothers pushing each other in the creek. They began to experiment with giving a storyline to their home movies.

As the children grew, these became elaborate productions of intrigue and adventure. Hester would paint sets and make costumes for pirates, cowboys or Russian spies. Rick would construct props. Joanne did everything else – writing, directing, shooting. She even acted, as soon as she could teach her oldest brother, Chris, to hold the camera steady.

Her parents were not thrilled that their daughter was using her skills in pornography. But after many long discussions around the woodstove, they eventually became reconciled to the fact that Joanne had to follow her muse and do what she found fulfilling. After all, wasn't life a constant search for the meaning of existence and self-expression? And who were they to say where Joanne's particular karma would lead her?

Joanne felt drained by the time the radio program ended. She was also hungry, having come to the studio right from class. She hadn't even had time to grab a frozen yogurt or slice of pizza to sustain her. She grabbed her bag and shook hands with Phil. After thanking the engineer and the PA, she excused herself as graciously and quickly as she could.

It seemed to her an eternity passed by while she

waited for the elevator. But then, the Pru Tower was more than fifty floors tall. Most of all, she wanted to avoid Ben. He had seemed to enjoy the show – as well he should have, since the majority of callers had taken his side. Still, something troubled her about him, and she simply wasn't prepared to deal with it on an empty stomach.

The elevator finally opened in front of her. She was happy to see that it was an express after the top twenty floors. She got in and leaned against the back wall with relief. But just as the doors were closing, Ben came running full-tilt from the studio and jumped in.

"We've gotta stop meeting like this," he said, obviously in a great mood.

Joanne tried to ignore him as people got on and off the elevator on the top floors. But for a few floors before it turned into an express, they were alone, and Ben tried to break the silence.

"Hey, c'mon. You can talk to me," said Ben. "The pleasure's all mine."

Joanne turned and stared at him. Suddenly, in her mind's eye, Ben sprouted a goatee, sunglasses, and a hundred pounds of junk jewelry.

"Mr. Porter," she said coolly, "I don't know what your game is, but I'd bet a year's tuition that you're the same sleazebag who hired me to make that film."

Ben was caught totally off guard. He had thought he was home free with Joanne. "Ms. Taylor ... Joanne ..."

"It's Ms. Taylor to you!"

"Ms. Taylor, then. Can we go somewhere and talk? I like you, and I'd like to be friends."

"Friends?!" shouted Joanne as the express elevator and their stomachs dropped from the thirtieth floor. "You deceived me!"

Now it was Ben's turn to feign indignation.

"When the town's number one porno director tells me that she does an occasional 'independent film,' I think that limits the amount of moral outrage she's allowed."

Joanne turned away from him, partly to hide a smile in spite of herself, as the elevator doors opened onto the lobby.

"You have a point," she admitted.

They stepped out of the elevator and exited the building onto the Bolyston Street Plaza.

"Look, I'm starving. How about we go get something to eat and you can tell the town's number one porno director why the town's number one porno fighter is financing her."

As they walked down Newbury Street toward Kenmore Square, Joanne and Ben didn't talk about what was most on their minds. Ben wasn't sure what he could actually tell her, and Joanne was enjoying the fact that she had him on the spot and he knew it. Their talk, therefore, was mainly about the restaurants they were passing and what kind of food to have, whether to go for Thai, Middle Eastern, Chinese or seafood.

They couldn't come to an agreement, so just kept walking. As they crossed Mass Ave and passed Steve's

Ice Cream, they noticed an empty table in the front corner, and absolutely no one in line. They didn't need to discuss this one, but both, like lemmings to the sea, jumped straight in.

Once inside, Joanne couldn't decide on the best choice for dinner, so Ben gave his order first: carob rum raisin ice cream, Heath Bar and Oreo mix-ins, with hot fudge and strawberries.

"Yuck, that's disgusting!"

"I don't eat this stuff very often," Ben said, by way of explanation, "so when I do, I gotta do it right."

Joanne felt sick just looking at it, as the young man behind the counter topped Ben's sundae off with a huge mound of whipped cream.

"AND whipped cream?!"

"That's the whole point," said Ben. "The ice cream is just a whipped cream delivery system."

"It's obscene! Not to mention about a hundred thousand calories. UGH! I can't even stand to look at it!"

"And what can I get for you?" asked the server, enjoying the conversation.

"Just Coffee. And I guess a small coffee ice cream. Maybe a little hot fudge and a few nuts on top," said Joanne, adding smugly, "but hold the whipped cream."

"Would you like marshmallow sauce instead?" asked the obliging young man.

"Sure, that sounds good."

"Marshmallow?" groaned Ben. "You talk about me! Marshmallow on hot fudge? Now THAT'S obscene!"

"But mine is dinner," said Joanne.

"It's a real balanced meal, all right."

"Sure it is," she said. "I have something from each of the basic food groups – coffee, chocolate, nuts, and marshmallow."

They made their way to the empty table they had spotted through the window and put their food down. Ben went back and grabbed plastic spoons, paper napkins and cups of water from the dispensers at the end of the counter and brought them to the table. They ate in silence for a few minutes, until Joanne couldn't stand it any longer.

"Okay, Benjamin Porter. Time to come clean. What's going on?"

"Well, it's like this, see ..." Ben stammered, not having figured out yet what he was going to tell her.

"The truth, Buster!" Joanne said, waving a spoonful of coffee-hot-fudge-nuts-and-marshmallow at him in a threatening manner.

"Okay, okay!" said Ben, pushing her spoon away with his spoon. "Just don't wave that thing around when it's loaded!"

Joanne looked at the ice cream dribbling from her spoon and laughed, realizing how silly the situation was. Ben was relieved. He decided he couldn't lie to her.

"All right. The truth. Here it is. The movie is part of our fundraising drive."

Joanne leaned back in her chair and eyed him with serious skepticism, threatening him again with her loaded spoon.

"Do you expect me to believe that?"

"It IS the truth. I swear!"

"You're making a porn ..."

"SSHHH!" Ben whispered, looking around nervously, but not seeing anyone listening to them.

Joanne leaned into the table and lowered her voice to a whisper.

"You're making a dirty movie in order to stamp them out?!"

"Ah, yeah," Ben admitted, "and the funny thing is, we're actually pulling it off!"

"I have to admit, it IS pretty funny. Was it your idea?"

"Not entirely," said Ben. "I'm essentially the office manager. I work for them. I was telling you the truth about that."

"So, if you just work for them, how do you feel about it yourself? I mean, here you are, having ice cream with the enemy ..."

"Enemy?" said Ben with a chuckle. "You just don't know any better."

"Come on, really," Joanne insisted. "I want to know where you stand personally."

"Personally?" said Ben. "Porno films don't do anything for me personally. I think they're kinda boring, actually. But then, I haven't seen any of your other Oscarwinning movies."

"I only do them for the money," Joanne blurted out. "Don't you think I'd be doing other films if I could break in? I'd certainly never PAY to see one of them, Lord knows, but if that's what people want to see, I really don't see the harm in it."

"What about all the studies claiming porno flicks cause rape and incest and the like?" said Ben. He couldn't help trying to put her on the defensive.

"For every study like that there's at least one other saying the films do more good than harm by relieving tension. Studies never prove anything except that the researcher needs more funding for further studies."

As if tacitly declaring a draw in the discussion, they turned back to their sundaes, which were rapidly melting into shapeless brown blobs. Ben took a few bites, then started chuckling to himself again.

"What's so funny?" asked Joanne, preparing to defend herself again.

"I was just thinking how crazy this is, our being here together. We seem to be coming from the opposite directions and ending up in the same place."

"What do you mean?" she asked, puzzled, not sure whether she could safely drop her guard again or not.

"Just that you look like you're pro-porno in your work, and I look anti in mine. Yet we both kinda stand on the middle ground, in reality."

"Does that mean you don't hold my shady past against me?"

"No," said Ben, "as long as you can deal with my present. I like these people I work with, and I'm committed to helping them. I may not share their passion for their beliefs, but I believe in their believing ...."

"And I can believe in your believing in their believing," said Joanne.

"Can you believe I want to see you again?" asked Ben.

Joanne smiled, then became serious.

"Will that be okay? I mean, I don't have anything to lose, but what if people start seeing us together? Your scheme is so wild I doubt anyone would guess it in a million years. But still, if I found you out ..."

"Leave that to me," said Ben. "I'll think of something."

"Okay," said Joanne, only too happy to leave it to him. "How's your ice cream?"

"Terrific! Want a taste?"

He passed his bowl to her and she helped herself to a tentative spoonful of the gooey mess.

"Yum! That's surprisingly good," she said, digging her spoon in for another, bigger scoop. "Want some of mine?"

Ben made a face, but reached over and took a spoonful.

"Marshmallow. Not bad!"

Chapter 11

B y the Fourth of July weekend, the response to the membership mailing had surpassed even Franklin's highest expectations. The movie was now in its fifth week at the BeauX Arts, and the protests outside were growing daily. Boston was naturally in a state of frenzy at this time of year, with a host of activities culminating in the Boston Pops concert and fireworks at the Hatch Shell on the Esplanade. The whole city came out to celebrate the glorious victory for democracy and freedom, if not liberty and justice for all.

Massachusetts, of course, laid particular claim to the holiday as the state in which the Revolution started. The good citizens of Boston still felt it was their duty to exercise their individual rights in the face of authority, as evidenced in the popular recall of a required seatbelt law of a few years ago, and the seemingly non-binding nature of the traffic rules. For the festivities, the city's population was swelled by every friend and relative the residents could stuff into their townhouses, apartments and condos.

The entire D.A.M.N.! membership had turned out for the weekend's protest, each bringing their houseguests along for the fun. Adding to their ranks were other organizations who were either against various evils or pro their own definitions of "clean living." One group carried a sign announcing they were "Women Against Pornography But Not Erotic Art." Their leader, Millie Forman, had temporary possession of the soapbox:

"We have to take the law into our own hands and shut down these places of filth," Millie yelled into a megaphone. "We must do away with this masculine-dominated pornography and replace it with erotic art that glorifies women's sexuality."

"What's the difference?" came the voice of a heckler in the crowd.

Millie lowered her megaphone and looked him in the eye.

"Listen, buddy. If WE don't like it, it's pornography!"

Shaking his head, the man sauntered into the theater.

A thin, weathered man with a long white beard began walking up and down in front of the protesters. He wore a sandwich board that one could spend half an hour trying to read.

"Sinners!" he yelled to no one and everyone. "Now is the time to repent. The dark days of judgment are at hand. This is what Rome was like before the fall!"

A group on a "Walking Tour of Boston" marched by.

"This is the quaint and colorful Combat Zone," the young guide explained. "It's second only to New York's Times Square as the most notorious adult entertainment district in the Northeast. We are now passing the historic BeauX Arts Cinema, which has generated a great deal of local interest as the film *Adam and Eve and Rhonda and Joey* goes into its second month amidst the protests we are now walking through. Those of you who would like to take your rest stop now can rejoin the group at four o'clock in the historic Filene's Basement, just a few blocks from here."

Several of the men ditched their wives and hurried into the theater as the guide moved the remnants of his group off toward Downtown Crossing.

The D.A.M.N.! picketers actually looked surprisingly reserved by comparison to the rest of the crowd. They held their position off to one side and handed out leaflets.

"Write the Mayor! Write the DA!" Ben yelled at passersby. "Demand that this film be shut down."

"This is beginning to resemble a three-ring circus," said Franklin, as Ben handed out several flyers to a group of young women strolling by.

Margaret, standing with Franklin and Ben, was getting more and more annoyed. "These people could give censorship a bad name!" she said, waving an arm toward Millie.

"Don't worry, Margaret," said Ben. "This publicity is great. Look!"

He pointed to a TV camera crew getting out of their van and coming toward them.

"There's Tim Willard. We're going to make the six o'clock news!"

Tim Willard was one of the most popular newsmen

in town, in part because he shunned the anchor desk for hard-hitting field work. It also didn't hurt that he was drop-dead gorgeous.

"All right, who's in charge here?" Tim asked as he approached the crowd.

The mass of humanity rushed toward him. Giving a quick fake left, Tim did an end run to the right and ended up in the D.A.M.N.! corner. Ben saw his opportunity. Grabbing Margaret by the elbow, he stepped up to the newsman.

"Hello, Mr. Willard. I'm Ben Porter of Decency and Morality Now!. This is Margaret O'Leary, our president," he said, gently pushing her in front.

"Great," said Tim. "we'll set up here."

His cameraman and soundman came up quickly, took their readings on light and ambient sound, and called, "Rolling." Tim, standing next to Margaret, faced the camera, and spoke into his microphone.

"I'm standing in front of the BeauX Arts Cinema in Downtown Boston, where protesters are urging the banning of the film, *Adam and Eve and Rhonda and Joey.* I'm joined by Margaret O'Leary and Ben Porter of Decency and Morality Now! an antipornography organization spearheading the protest drive on this film. Mrs. O'Leary, what do you hope to accomplish here today?"

Margaret started to draw back as Tim held the mike in front of her. Ben smiled and gave her a little nudge on the arm, out of camera view.

"Uh, the people of Boston are simply saying 'enough

is enough,' and if everyone who is sick of this tide of filth would write our elected officials, they would be forced to respond."

"Are you conducting a formal letter-writing campaign, as well?" asked Tim into his mike, before sticking it in Ben's face.

"Indeed, we are," said Ben obligingly. "We need everyone to urge the city to take action."

The cameraman zoomed in on Tim for a closeup.

"It's been twenty years or more since a film was banned in Boston. Whether this campaign succeeds or not remains to be seen. Reporting live from in front of the BeauX Arts Cinema, I'm Tim Willard."

Joanne and Ben hadn't seen each other since the night of the radio show. They had both been busy cramming for finals and registering for summer quarter. Joanne was beginning to be sorry that she had left the arrangements for getting together again up to Ben.

What if he developed cold feet after all, she thought. She had been watching the growing protest movement against her film, and consoled herself by thinking that Ben might have been kept busy with it. Still, she found herself thinking about him more than she wished.

The day after the Fourth, when the city was starting to settle down again in the summer's heat and humidity, Joanne stopped by The Library after class for a cup of coffee. As she slumped down at her usual table, in a back corner next to the stacks, she heard a familiar voice call her name.

"Ben?" she answered, not bothering to conceal her delight.

"Hi, there! I was hoping you'd be in here today."

"I saw you and Margaret on the news last night," Joanne told the stack of books from which the voice of Ben was coming.

"Oh, yeah? How'd I look?"

"Big as life! That's the problem. The whole world will recognize you now!"

"My sister's been getting calls from her friends all day," said the voice, "which is why I'm not showing my face."

"This is serious, Ben. It means we can't risk being seen together by ANYBODY!"

As if to confirm her fears, Joanne looked around and saw a man at the next table staring at her seemingly one-sided conversation. She picked up one of her books.

"Sorry," she said. "Just ... ah ... reading aloud."

"Don't worry," said Ben from the other side of the stacks.

"What do you mean don't worry?"

Noticing the man still looking at her, Joanne held her book up and began to talk in a voice that one would use when reading aloud.

"Do you want to see me or not?"

"Of course, I want to see you!" answered Ben.

"Then how can you tell me not to worry?"

"You're raising your voice ..."

"I'm not raising ..." Joanne looked up at the man watching her. She smiled and shrugged a "sorry." Then, whispering into the book again, she resumed her rant.

"How can you tell me not to worry?!"

"We can meet like this," said Ben.

"I don't want to meet like this!"

"Why not?" asked Ben, obviously toying with her now.

"Because I want to SEE you, okay?"

"You can see me," he said.

"How, without our being recognized together?"

Ben took a couple of books off the stacks and stuck his face into the hole across from Joanne. She saw him and laughed, causing the man at the nearby table to get up in disgust, take his tray and move to the far side of the room.

"Your place or mine?" said Ben, sporting his producer's garb of goatee, sunglasses and three pounds of junk jewelry.

Even though Joanne's apartment was closer, they decided to take the T to Ben's on Charles Street so he could change his clothes. Ben offered to get her a cab when she wanted to go home. This was fine with Joanne. She certainly didn't want to be seen with Ben in his producer's getup in her own building.

She suggested they board separate cars and walk on different sides of the street to DeLuca's market on Charles Street. There, Joanne bought cheese and crackers, and Ben purchased some grapes.

Using utmost discretion, Ben had given Joanne his address so she could cross the street ahead of him and wait in the doorway. He was enjoying the intrigue of their friendship. It certainly would be a bummer for them to be seen together, but it also heightened the erotic suspense for him.

Ben waited a few moments in front of DeLuca's, pretending to inspect the pomegranates. Then he jogged across the street to his building. He unlocked the door into the lobby, and Joanne hurried up to the top of the stairs. Ben waited a moment and then followed her up to unlock his apartment door and deadbolt.

Joanne was surprised at how neat the apartment was. It may have been a bit sparse on furnishings, but she definitely saw potential. One entered into a small foyer with a little table against the wall. She could see a bedroom off to the left and a living room to the right, with only a couch and end table, a bookshelf and a small desk. Straight ahead was the kitchen, large enough to hold a small table and two chairs in the middle.

"You can put your things down here," he said, pointing to the table in the foyer."

He dropped his backpack on the floor beside it and picked up their two bags from DeLuca's. He took them into the kitchen and put them down on the counter. Then he took out a chilled bottle of rose from the refrigerator.

"C'mon," he said, as he handed her the wine and two goblets from the cupboard.

"Where are we going?" she asked.

"To my terrace," he said, unlocking and opening the tall kitchen window, the bottom of which was only a few feet above the floor.

Ben crawled out onto the fire escape, then turned around and took the wine and glasses from Joanne. He set them down on the wide window ledge and helped her out. The night was balmy and breezy, and if they stretched their necks, they could see the moonlight shining on the Charles River beyond the rooftops below them.

"Your apartment is really nice," said Joanne, after they were comfortably seated on the window ledge and Ben had poured them each a glass of wine.

"You sound surprised," said Ben. "What did you expect?"

"Um, I don't know, clothes all around, dishes in the sink. You know, the usual bachelor pad kind of thing."

"I'm a business student. We're very orderly."

"Getting in practice for when you'll be juggling the books, huh?"

"I'm prepared for an unexpected visit from the IRS or my mother at any time."

Joanne suddenly shivered as the breeze turned refreshingly cool.

"You're cold. Shall we go back in?"

Ben raised the window and they crawled back into the warmth of the apartment.

"Would you do me a favor?" asked Joanne, as they carried their glasses into the living room.

"Anything. I'm yours!" Ben replied.

"Would you get out of that ridiculous outfit?"

"Your wish is my command," said Ben.

He set his glass down quickly on the desk. Then he dropped his pants and took off his shirt, leaving only the fake beard, the jewelry, and his Glen plaid boxer shorts.

"I didn't mean right here!" said Joanne, shocked.

"You're the director," he said, as he swept her into his arms and kissed her passionately. He started to ease them back onto the couch, but Joanne struggled against him. They dropped so abruptly onto the back of the sofa that it tumbled over, with the back hitting the floor and the feet sticking out.

"That's a new one for me," said Ben, laughing, oblivious to the fact that Joanne was not exactly going with the flow.

"Hey, come back here," he said, as she got up and ran toward the foyer.

"I'm outta here," Joanne said, picking up her things.

"I'm sorry about the couch," Ben said, coming over to stand between Joanne and the door. "It never could behave itself. But I have a bed in the other room that's a model of propriety – always stays just where I tell it to ..."

"I don't care about your furniture! Goodbye, Mr. Porter!" Joanne screamed at him, as she pushed past him and out the door.

"Hey, wait a minute," Ben called after her, grabbing his keys and running out to the landing. "I'm really sorry about the couch. You don't have to get so mad at a little thing like that."

"I'm not mad at your stupid couch!" Joanne yelled from the second-floor landing as Ben hit the third.

"Then would you come back up here and tell it? I think it deserves to be told to its face."

Joanne stopped halfway down the next flight of stairs in disbelief. *What in the hell is wrong with him?* she thought.

"Why don't you just go and ... put some clothes on!" was all she could manage to say.

With that, she ran down to the lobby.

"Only if you come back up here and talk to me," yelled Ben, reaching the bottom just as Joanne ran out the front door onto Charles Street.

Ben followed her out and caught up with her on the corner. Joanne, mortified by the sight of Ben in public in only his boxers, not to mention the disapproving looks they were getting from the well-bred Beacon Hill passersby, retraced her steps and ducked back into the doorway.

"Will you please just let me go?" she pleaded, as Ben crammed in with her.

"Will you please just let me say I'm sorry? I honestly don't know for what yet, but I am sorry. Please come back up."

Suddenly a ton of bricks fell on Ben's head. "I promise I won't touch you," he said softly.

"Well," said Joanne, at ease now that he seemed to understand her anger. "You don't have to go THAT far."

By all rights, Joanne thought to herself as she followed Ben back into his apartment, she ought to just leave for good. But she liked him, despite the fact that he could be Jack the Ripper. Still, it just didn't figure, somehow, and so she stayed.

Even Ben was a little out of breath from running up and down his stairs, so they sat down on the floor with their backs to the bottom of the upturned couch.

"I guess I'm just not what you expected. Sorry," said Joanne.

"You have nothing to be sorry about. At least, you don't need to apologize to me. I wasn't exactly behaving like the paragon of Decency and Morality Now!"

"It's just that every man I meet seems to think that because I make those movies, I'll jump into bed with everyone."

Now it was Ben's turn to get embarrassed.

"I'm sorry ... I mean ... I didn't ..." he stammered, unsure how he was going to get out of this one.

"See? I'm right, aren't I?" said Joanne. "I guess it's a natural reaction – guilt by association. I thought you'd be different because of where you worked."

"Touché!" murmured Ben, dropping his head back on the couch.

"But that's why you invited me here, too, isn't it? Maybe I should go."

She started to get up, but Ben, rising to his knees, gently took her hand.

"Joanne, please. That's not why I asked you here. I promise. I didn't even think of it until just that moment when you told me to take off my clothes."

"You didn't?" said Joanne, feigning outrage and getting to her feet.

She picked up a couch pillow and hit him on the head. Ben, in turn, grabbed her around the knees, bringing her to the floor and tickling her.

"You win! UNCLE!" cried Joanne.

He stopped, but still held her down by her arms.

"So, now, tell me the rules of the game," he said, with a note of seriousness in his voice. "What am I supposed to do next?"

"Letting me up wouldn't hurt."

"Oh, sorry," said Ben, quickly releasing her.

She sat up, but continued to look at him. Ben gently touched her cheek.

"Why is it that I still want to kiss you?"

"Oh, Ben," she said, "It just has to be very, very right before I'll ... I'll ... and it so rarely ever is. It's just too soon."

He leaned over and kissed her gently on the forehead, then held both her hands and looked her in the eyes.

"I'm really sorry, Joanne. I don't know what got into me. I'm usually not the kind of guy to force myself on a woman." He had a sudden thought and dropped her hands. "And I promised I wouldn't touch you!"

Joanne laughed. "Yes, you did, but it's okay. I'll release you from that promise, at least a little bit."

"Then will you stay if I get dressed?" Ben asked.

"Yes, if you'll do one other thing for me."

"What's that?"

"Take off that silly beard!"

Ben got up and went into the bedroom to change into a t-shirt and jeans. He couldn't believe how he had acted tonight. He knew he had come close to blowing it totally with Joanne, and he liked her so much. It must have been the wine, he thought. Or maybe it was the sense of intrigue, of "forbidden love," that was so intoxicating.

Then a much darker thought crossed his mind: Could it be that his recent foray into the realm of porno was actually having an erotic effect on him? Could porn actually be a danger to society, like some people say?

Not wanting to go too far down that track right then, he allowed his mind to entertain another excuse: *Maybe it was just my sleazebag costume. Yeah, that's it. I was getting into the role. I'd better come up with another disguise.*

Then he had another thought as he stuffed his costume in a gym bag and threw it in the closet. It had been a long time since he'd had a girlfriend, what with school and work occupying his time and energy. Yet it had always been his style to take things slowly. Most of the women he liked preferred it that way, too. The AIDS thing had certainly put a damper on general "messing around," anyway. He much preferred waiting until the woman was ready to come to him – much more exciting to have a woman you've been gallantly courting for several months suddenly jump your bones. *Yes*, he thought, *the threat of AIDS aside, you miss so much romance if you move too fast.*

But Joanne! She was different than anyone he had dated before. Who would have figured HER for a go-slow girl? Not that he didn't long to sleep with her, but he wanted to be with her so much that he could actually see spending the night just holding her and kissing her. Then he caught sight of himself in the mirror on the back of his door. He looked good, except for the goatee still attached to his chin. He could forget even kissing her if he went out like that, he laughed to himself as he yanked it off.

Ben came back into the living room via the kitchen so he could pick up the wine bottle. Joanne came back in from the bathroom where she had gone to comb her hair. This, or course, was the automatic response common to most women in the aftermath of battle.

"Some spokesman for decency and morality I'VE

turned out to be," said Ben, when they were once more settled on the floor against the upturned couch.

"Maybe we should trade jobs," Joanne suggested, obviously more relaxed now that Ben looked like Ben again.

"I have the outfit for it, huh?"

"Don't remind me!"

"Would you like some more wine?" Ben asked.

"Sure," Joanne answered, reaching up for her glass that was on the end table next to the couch. She couldn't see that next to the glass was a stack of letters and envelopes, all of which came flying down on her as she pulled her glass off the table.

"What's all this?" she asked, as she picked up a letter and turned it right-side up so she could read it.

"Huh?" said Ben, who had been crawling over to the other side of the room for his own glass on the desk. He turned around to see Joanne extricating herself from his correspondence.

"That's the mailing for the letter-writing campaign. We're going to make your movie the most controversial film to hit Boston in twenty-five years."

"Hear, hear!" said Joanne, raising her glass. "To controversy!"

"To controversy!" said Ben, crawling back and clinking his glass against hers. "Shall we drink to it?"

"Might as well make it an official toast," said Joanne, holding her glass up so he could pour more wine into it. "Do you really think it's going to work?"

"It's already working!" said Ben, raising his glass to hers again and then taking a drink.

He suddenly turned serious, as a new thought came to him.

"This is going to make you notorious. I hope that's not going to be a problem for you and your career."

"In this racket, there's no such thing as bad publicity. I need to make a name for myself. The more controversial the movie, the better my chances of getting out of porno for good."

"That'll make Margaret happy."

"Why?"

"She's afraid that everyone involved in this film has sold their soul to the devil."

"No. Just to a sleazebag producer," Joanne said, leaning over and kissing Ben tenderly.

Delighted with the new turn of events, Ben kissed her in return. Then, forcing himself to keep his libido under control, he embraced her, holding her close to him. He kissed the side of her head. Joanne suddenly pulled her head away from his shoulder so she could look him in the face.

"Since you've given my career such a boost, the least I can do is help you do it."

"You actually want to help us?"

"Sure. Your success is my success. Francis Coppola started out doing nudie films and ended up making *The Godfather*."

"And what do you want to do?" said Ben, tickling her again, *"The Godmother?"*

Joanne groaned. "That's terrible! Just for that, you can go get the cheese and crackers. And don't forget to wash the grapes. I'll stuff the envelopes," she said, giving him a little kiss on the nose, "and YOU can lick the stamps!"

Chapter 12

District Attorney Burton Halloran was one of those old-style politicians who had finally gotten himself into an office where he could delegate most of his responsibilities. Not that he didn't have higher ambitions, of course. Mayor might be too much work, and he hated the bother of campaigning. But a nice safe, appointed-for-life judgeship, that could be the ticket. And wouldn't he look dapper in the black robe, too!

The walls of Burton's office were covered with plaques and awards, and photos of him receiving plaques and awards. Everything else in the room – the desk, the floor, the couch and lamp table – was covered with mountains of letters demanding that the DA crack down on pornography. In particular, the letters called for a ban on a certain movie playing at the BeauX Arts Cinema. It was to handle this crisis that he had called in Albert, his assistant, who usually could keep things in the DA's office humming along beautifully without having to bother the DA at all.

"Don't these people have anything better to do?" Burton asked his able young assistant. "I've got letters from everyone but the Cardinal himself!"

"Didn't you see the Cardinal's letter?" asked Albert. "I put it right on top."

He rummaged around through the pile on Burton's desk, then spied it on the floor and stooped to pick it up.

"Here it is. Shall I read it?"

Burton waved his hand in resignation.

"It's a copy of a sermon he's preparing on sin in Boston and how our officials are failing to respond," said Albert. He began to read, "If the sewers were to overflow on Beacon Hill, our elected officials would see to it that appropriate action was taken. Shouldn't we expect even quicker response when our moral sewers are emptying themselves onto our city streets?"

"Moral sewers?" Burton wasn't at all sure he liked the Cardinal's metaphor.

"We have to do something, sir. Uncle Jim is challenging the Governor in the primary this fall," Albert explained. "He can't afford to have the Cardinal calling this city a hotbed of sin."

"What do the Mayor's problems have to do with me?" Burton whined. "I've got my own campaign to worry about."

"His Honor was over for dinner last night and we were talking about it. Now suppose we were to stage a raid. Shut down that film they're all complaining about."

"Why bother?" asked Burton. "The reason we don't prosecute these cases is that we can't win. The judges just dismiss them on some technicality, like that law they threw out because it was ..." The word was on the tip of his tongue, but he couldn't quite spit it out.

"Because it was unconstitutional?" Albert offered.

"That's the one."

"Uncle Jim has thought of that, sir. He wants you to try this case, but he expects you to lose it. That way he can accuse the Governor of appointing judges who are morally lax while promising to put men of your caliber on the bench."

The kid was finally making sense, thought Burton. "I've always wanted a nice quiet probate court I could call my own," he said, knowing Albert would take that information back to his Uncle Jim, the Mayor. "Just wills and codicils and not a thief or a prostitute around for miles."

"And no re-election campaigns to worry about, either, huh?" said Albert, who had been around politicians all of his thirty-two years and knew an opening when he saw one, "... judges being appointed for life and all."

"I like the way you think, young man," said Burton. "Are there any more at home like you?"

"Four brothers and two sisters. You'll meet them all at the birthday party and fundraiser Uncle Jim is throwing for Grandma next week. Have you reserved your seats yet?"

"Uh, no, not yet," Burton said, knowing he was on the spot but having no idea how he got there.

"Then you're in luck," said Albert, with the innocence of a Boy Scout selling raffle tickets to send a kid to summer camp. "I happen to have a book of tickets on me. It's only five hundred dollars for two, and it's for a good cause."

"What cause?" asked Burton, in a last-ditch effort to save his soul, not to mention five hundred dollars.

"Uncle Jim's campaign."

Burton knew his ship had just sunk, so he picked up his checkbook, wrote out the check and handed it to Albert.

"Who's going to prosecute this case?" Burton asked, as Albert gave him the tickets, pocketed the check and turned to leave. "We have a good team here. How can you be sure we'll lose?"

"Leave that to me, sir," said Albert, with confidence. "I've got just the man."

Albert left the DA's office with a light step. *How I love this job,* he said to himself, although managing Burton Halloran wasn't much of a challenge. Still, it was good practice. After all, he was the heir apparent to his uncle, the mayor, being the oldest boy of all the cousins. It was fortunate for him Uncle Jim had produced only daughters. They might all go to Harvard Law School, but a woman be elected Mayor of Boston? Even in this day and age, not bloody likely.

The next stop on Albert's agenda today was "The Bullpen," a large room down the hall where the junior attorneys in the DA's office worked. At one of the eight desks, back in the corner, sat Douglas Finkel, a recent recruit to the staff. Doug was only one year out of New York University law school, where he had been a classmate of Albert's cousin Michael. He had some impressive qualifications – Law Review, Democrat, hard worker, and best of all, non-Irish so no threat to Albert's political ambitions.

Albert marched straight to Doug and pushed some files away so he could sit on the corner of the desk.

"Congratulations!" he said, grabbing Doug's hand and shaking it.

"Huh?" Doug looked up, startled.

"You're getting the big case. The Old Man decided you were ready for it."

"Really?" Doug asked, suddenly excited. "I'm getting to prosecute Sammy the Torch?"

"Well, no ..." said Albert.

"The Mattapan Mugger?" Doug took a second guess.

"Not exactly."

Doug gave a sigh. "The poor sucker who nabbed your uncle for speeding?"

"The man was drunk and disorderly," said Albert defensively. "He frisked the Mayor and was getting ready to cuff him when the Police Commissioner woke up in the back seat!"

"I knew it," said Doug, shaking his head. "It IS the cop."

"No, no. But it's another very important case. The DA agrees you're just the man for the job. He wants your youthful zeal to handle it."

"So what is it already?" Doug was getting exasperated with the guessing game.

"Douglas," said Albert, placing his hand on the young attorney's shoulder. "The DA wants you to raid the BeauX Arts Cinema."

"WHAT!" Doug's reaction could probably have been

heard all the way to Brookline. "A PORNO case! I won't do it!"

Doug was still protesting to Albert as they entered police headquarters.

"I won't DO it!" he was saying for the millionth time as officer Bob Connolly came into the interrogation room and was introduced to Doug.

This small room was set aside for the DA's use for private conferences on official business.

"Doug, will you calm down?"

Albert knew he would get his way in the end, but this kid could sure be annoying in the meantime, he thought. The three men sat down around a small table, and Albert turned to the policeman.

"So, Officer Connolly. What's the next step?" he asked, deciding to ignore Doug entirely.

"I don't have to tell you gentlemen that we need probable cause to get a warrant for the raid," said the officer.

"A RAID! My professors at NYU would be very proud of me, yes indeed!" Doug whined, while Albert ignored him, and Officer Connolly looked at him with curiosity.

"What we do is accompany someone from the DA's office, I guess that would be you, Mr. Finkel, and we view the alleged film," he said, still looking at Doug as if to figure him out.

"It's definitely a film, Officer Connolly," said Albert. "What's alleged is that it's obscene."

"Obscene!" wailed Doug. "How am I ever going to face my friends in the ACLU again!"

"I'll be wired with a micro-cassette recorder, with a microphone taped to my wrist," said Connolly, taking a cue from Albert and ignoring Doug. "I'll tape a blow-by-blow description of the perpetration of the alleged acts."

"That tape before a friendly judge should be more than enough," said Albert.

"What if it's not?" said Doug. "Maybe we should start boiling some oil, just in case!"

"Douglas," said Albert in a condescending tone. "I don't think you have the right attitude toward this."

"I joined the DA's staff to fight crime," he answered, "not to raid movie theaters!"

"It's not all that bad, sir," said Connolly, trying to be reassuring.

Doug snapped his head around to face the officer. "And I suppose you enjoy your work, Officer Connolly?"

"It's a dirty job, sir," said the policeman, with a totally straight face, "but somebody's got to do it."

Doug looked at him for a moment. Connolly's expression never flinched.

"All right," the young attorney said with a sigh of resignation. "Let's get this over with."

As Officer Connolly changed out of his uniform into plainclothes, and Doug tried to prepare himself to go against his conscience for the sake of his job, Joanne was looking for Ben in Quincy Market. The latest heat wave had broken the night before with a ferocious thunderstorm, and the refreshing breeze from the sea had moved off what was left of the humidity.

Because Quincy Market was just below Government Center, it attracted the lunch crowd from the offices, not just tourists. On this beautiful midsummer day, it was crowded, and everyone was having a good time in the circus-like atmosphere. Mimes, musicians and magicians were performing in every open space. Each one was surrounded by children and adults alike.

Joanne looked in the center of each circle, but it was not until she spotted a bouquet of huge mylar daisy balloons that she knew she'd found her man.

"I have to admit," she said, approaching the balloons, "this one beats the sleazebag look. But do you have to take your disguises to such extremes?"

From the middle of the bouquet, a painted-white mime face appeared. Ben, dressed in black, bowed and handed Joanne a balloon with a mime-style flourish.

"C'mon, you can talk to me," said Joanne, laughing.

Ben only mimed, pointing to his lips, shaking his head, and handing her another balloon. Joanne was amused but annoyed at the same time.

"That's the point of the disguise, right? So we can be together – TALK together – without being recognized."

116

Ben mimed again and tried to hand her another balloon. Frustrated, Joanne refused to hold the string. The balloon sailed off into the sky, with Ben looking after it.

"Okay, Joannie," he said, "I just thought it would be fun to stay in character."

He handed her another balloon.

"Peace?"

"Peace," she said, with a bow, adding this balloon to the other two still in her hand.

"Why, hello Benjamin."

Joanne and Ben were both startled at the greeting.

"Mrs. Abbott," said Ben, as Joanne turned around to see who behind her had recognized him. "What are YOU doing here, I mean ... hello, I ..."

"Very clever, Benjamin," said the proper Mrs. Abbott. "Is this another one of your business school projects?"

"Yes ... I mean, no ..."

"Oh, dear," said Mrs. Abbott with sympathy. "You're not out fundraising, are you? I must speak to Franklin about this. You shouldn't have to beg in the streets for operating funds."

"But ... but ..."

"Never you mind, dear. I'll handle this."

Mrs. Abbott smiled at Joanne as if apologizing for interrupting their business transaction and bustled off into the crowd.

"Another great disguise, huh 'Benjamin'?!" Joanne said with a laugh. "Who was that?"

"Franklin's mother!"

"Oh, great!"

"I'd better get over to the protest, anyway."

He gave her a kiss, getting white on her face. Handing her the rest of the balloons, he ran off toward City Hall.

"Ben, wait!" yelled Joanne after him. "What am I going to do with these? I have to go to class!"

Ben ran back, took one balloon from her, kissed her, and ran off again. He leaped up the City Hall stairs three at a time, then ran across Cambridge Street and through Downtown Crossing to the Combat Zone.

Joanne stood there, holding the balloons, looking after him, stunned. Finally, she shook her head and laughed.

When Ben got to the BeauX Arts, the man with the sandwich board was still marching up and down. Many of the other groups had fallen by the wayside over the past month, however, and the protest ranks were growing thinner daily. Even some of the D.A.M.N.! faithful had turned in their placards and picked up their pens, assuring themselves that they were still doing their part just writing letters to the Mayor and DA. Unfortunately, the waning visibility of the protest movement was reflected in diminishing audiences for the film.

Ben stopped by the D.A.M.N.! office across the street to clean off his face and put on a shirt and tie. He then ran down the stairs and across the street to join Margaret and Franklin trying to drum up some interest in the protest and the film.

"Here, Margaret, this is for you," said Ben, handing her the single daisy balloon he had picked out of Joanne's hand at the last minute.

"Why, thank you, Ben," said Margaret. "Look, Franklin, it's a daisy. What's the occasion?"

"It's such a beautiful day, and I was passing through Quincy Market and couldn't resist," he told her. "Besides, we have reason to celebrate. Ernie told me we've already made back our initial investment. It's all gravy from now on."

"Not much of a crowd here today, though," said Franklin, looking around.

"Just give it time," said Ben. "It'll pick up again."

"I know this was my idea," said Franklin, "but from what you say, we've just broken even. If things don't pick up again, we'll be right back where we started, and ..."

"Oh, look," said Margaret, cutting him off. "There's my sister Helen's boy. Yoo-hoo, Bobby! Over here!" she yelled, waving.

Officer Connolly came up to Margaret. Doug, wearing sunglasses and a false moustache, hung back. He looked furtively around.

"Aunt Margaret!" Connolly said with surprise. "What are you doing here?"

"We're protesting this dirty movie. What are YOU doing here that your mother should know about?!"

Connolly took her aside.

"I can't tell you, Aunt Margaret. It's official police business. I'm sorry."

"I understand," said Margaret with a sigh. "Well, please give my regards to your mother."

"I'll do that, Aunt Margaret."

And with that, Officer Connolly turned and approached the ticket window.

"Bobby, maybe you can come over for dinner on Sunday," Margaret yelled after him, causing him to look around and suddenly turn almost as nervous as Doug.

"I'll give you a call," Connolly said, and hurried into the theater.

"What was that all about?" Franklin asked, as the two men disappeared into the den of sin.

"That's my sister Helen's boy. He's a policeman," Margaret answered with pride.

"A cop?" asked Ben, suddenly very interested.

"He's assigned to Vice."

"Do you suppose he's here on a raid?" asked Franklin, not sure whether he should be sad or glad about that possibility.

Ben, however, had no doubt.

"See? I knew we'd have a reason to celebrate. We'll be in court in no time!"

Just then, Margaret noticed something in the sky over Boston Common a block away.

"Look! There's a whole bouquet!"

Floating over the Common on the sea breeze were the rest of Ben's daisy balloons.

While Margaret, Franklin and Ben watched the balloons float higher in the sky until they finally disappeared over Cambridge, Officer Connolly and Doug crossed the darkened theater lobby on their way to the auditorium.

"Six dollars a ticket! That's outrageous!" Doug complained.

"Senior citizens get in for four," said his partner matter-of-factly. "Hold on, I want some popcorn," Connolly said as they passed the refreshments counter. "You want some?"

Doug was grossed out by the thought.

"Here?!" he exclaimed.

"I'm hungry," said the cop. "I didn't have time for lunch."

"But popcorn HERE? You don't know where it's been!"

While Doug was turning green at the thought of pornographic popcorn, Connolly ignored him and bought a jumbo bag and a Coke. Then the two undercover G-men entered the auditorium. The audience was sparse, with only a few patrons scattered around. Connolly picked seats in the center, toward the front, because Doug was having trouble seeing anything in the dimly lit theater but refused to remove his sunglasses.

"I've never been so embarrassed in my entire life," he said, slouching down in his seat.

"I take it you've never seen` one of these films," said Connolly, finding Doug an amusing, if irritating, companion.

"Of course not!"

"Then how do you know it's not obscene?"

"Because the whole idea of obscenity is ridiculous," said Doug smugly. "There's nothing inherently bad about showing sex in the movies."

"Sounds like you should be working for the other side," said Connolly, munching his popcorn.

Doug, finally feeling free to express his feelings, became carried away with his rhetoric. His voice was getting louder and louder.

"I'm on the side of free expression. I believe in the rights of all citizens to read whatever books they want and see whatever movies they choose. And who are WE to determine taste for anyone else?"

An empty candy box flew from six rows back and hit Doug squarely in the back of the head.

"You wanna pipe down in front?!" came a voice from the same direction.

"The public speaks, sir," said Officer Connolly.

With that, the houselights went out, the curtains opened, and the officer started his tape recorder.

"The first film is a preview of coming attractions," Connolly whispered into the recorder. "A nude female Caucasian is suspended from a trapeze while two nude male Caucasians, two nude male Blacks, and two nude females of Chinese extraction carry on a large snake ...."

"Omigod! Omigod!" was all Doug could manage to say as he slunk further and further into his seat.

Chapter 13

Doug Finkel didn't sleep at all that night. Dark visions of Biblical damnations did a devil's dance in his mind and soul, their naked, wraith-like forms crackling and bellowing in malevolent laughter in the midst of devouring flames.

Here he was, a proud native of New York City – Jewish, Democratic card-carrying member of the ACLU, though certainly not a Pinko-Commie-Fascist whatever. He had a firm commitment to the First Amendment. He believed – almost to the point of being Libertarian – in individual rights, including the right to read and see whatever one wanted to read and see. But he had never actually seen a porno film himself, nor hardly ever been near 42nd Street and Broadway. Now, his political religion was being tested, because – to state it simply – Doug Finkel had been grossed out.

He moved zombie-like through his morning bagel, cream cheese and black coffee, which in New York terms meant with sugar. He was barely conscious of riding the Green Line in from Coolidge Corner, or getting off at Government Center and crossing the Plaza into City Hall. He was still practically catatonic when Officer Connolly played the tape he had made during the movie for Albert.

"Fourteen bodies are writhing on the floor," came Connolly's voice into his subconscious, "while one of the women has her leg up on the couch. One of the men suddenly stands on his head in the middle of the group, and the woman pushes off the couch to somersault ..."

When he heard himself on the tape saying, "The horror! The horror! I can't believe this!" in ever increasing decibel levels, Doug began to return to conscious thought.

"I'm sorry, sir," said Connolly, as Albert turned off the tape in response to Doug's latest outburst. "Mr. Finkel apparently couldn't control his reactions. He was ready to raid the place right then and there."

"It was horrible," Doug muttered, his eyes wide-open and unblinking. "It was like Dante's Inferno. It was like a nightmare out of the Marquis De Sade. It was ...."

Officer Connolly interrupted him.

"It was a typical porno movie, sir."

"Typical?!" Doug exclaimed, shocked beyond comprehension. "Typical? You mean there are OTHERS like that?"

"Oh, sure," stated the officer matter-of-factly. "They all look pretty much the same after a while."

Doug's mission was now clear, and he turned to Albert.

"Let's get that warrant! Let's get this piece of filth out of circulation. I won't rest until the entire Combat Zone is shut down!"

"Doug," said Albert in the smooth tone of a born

politician. "I'm sure this has been a rough experience for you. Officer Connolly and I will arrange for the warrant. Why don't you go on home?"

"NO! I can't let another show go on! We're getting that warrant NOW!"

It took about an hour for the warrant to be issued. Doug and Officer Connolly were at the BeauX Arts in time to prevent the noontime showing. The press had been tipped off by Albert – Mr. Deep Throat of the DA's office – so Tim Willard was on the scene as Connolly emerged from the theater, film cannisters in hand.

This was cause for not a little celebration among D.A.M.N.! members, who were just straggling in for the day's demonstration. All were elated because an obnoxious film was at last under indictment, vindicating their position and actions. Everyone adjourned to Brigham's, where they engaged in a little "sin" of their own – ordering extra hot fudge and jimmies on their sundaes. Then, each member retired to his or her own home to await the six o'clock news.

As usual, Tim's report was thorough and to-the-point. He included interviews with both Doug and Ernie. Doug had insisted on joining in the raid, but then would be damned if he would set foot in that den of iniquity. He had returned enough to himself to be of some use to Tim.

Ernie had been tipped off by Peep Carlton the night before that Officer Connolly and an assistant DA had been seen entering the theater. He made sure to be at his office early so he would be available should the media call.

Now, Tim was drawing the battlelines for his viewers:

"The DA has obtained an indictment for obscenity against the film, *Adam and Eve and Rhonda and Joey*. This movie, which has had a controversial run for some twelve weeks here, is even now being confiscated by the police. Defending the film is Attorney Ernest McNerney."

The screen then cut to a tape of Tim's interview with Ernie:

"This is a flagrant violation of the First Amendment," said Ernie, looking steely-eyed into the camera, "and brings back times that we thought were over in Boston for good. I can assure you we will fight this latest case of censorship. This movie WILL be shown again."

After Ernie's bite, Tim came back on in front of the BeauX Arts, and the camera pulled out to reveal Doug standing beside him.

"With me now is Assistant District Attorney Douglas Finkel, who is spearheading this anti-smut drive. What happens now, Mr. Finkel?"

"Well, Tim," said Doug, "the film will be tried in court and I am certain that it will be found obscene. After that, anyone exhibiting it in Suffolk County will be prosecuted to the full extent of the law."

"What is the next step?" asked Tim.

"First, we must set the standards. Then I am confident we can get an injunction against showing this film in Boston."

The camera then zoomed back to Tim's handsome face.

"Tough words from the DA's office. Whether this campaign will influence or be influenced by the DA's tough re-election fight, only time will tell. This is Tim Willard, reporting from the BeauX Arts Cinema."

Across the street in the D.A.M.N.! office, Ben raised his plastic champagne glass for a toast.

"We did it!" he said.

"To success," toasted Franklin, as he and Margaret tapped Ben's glass with their own.

"So far so good," said Ben.

"Your nephew looked very nice on television last night," said Franklin, turning to Margaret. "Was that his first raid?"

"First one to make the news," she answered with a maternal smile.

"You should be very proud, Margaret," said Ben. "Now Ernie will defend the film, and when he wins, ticket sales will skyrocket!"

Margaret was suddenly uneasy.

"I just thought of something. Won't he have to reveal who made the film?" she asked. "He can't pretend it appeared out of nowhere!"

"Don't worry, Margaret," said Ben. "For once the law is on our side. They're just trying to get the film declared obscene, not to prosecute anyone. They'll only arrest people who SHOW the film, that is, IF it's found obscene, which is unlikely."

"That's right," said Franklin. "I've done a little checking up on this. All they'll do is show the movie to a jury, allow each side to call their expert witnesses, and then let the jury declare the film 'an important social-political statement, fully protected by the Constitution.' The judge will then thank the jury for perverting the will of our Founding Fathers and send them on their way."

"What expert witnesses?" Margaret wouldn't be happy if she couldn't be concerned about SOMETHING in this affair.

"The usual assortment of community leaders," said Ben. "English professors, film critics and clergymen – people guaranteed to confuse the jury and cancel each other out."

"Do you think WE might be called?" asked Margaret.

"Ernie wouldn't dare," said Ben.

"No, but Margaret has a point," said Franklin. "We may get called by the DA. We ARE the leading critics of the film, after all."

"Okay, but so what?" Ben argued. "If we're called, we'll tell the truth. The movie is an abomination. No one will ask us if we made it. The DA wouldn't dream of it, and Ernie would know better."

"Are you sure about that?" Margaret had to make sure there was still something to worry about. "I don't want to have to wait until visiting day at the jail to see my grandchildren!"

"Of course I'm sure!" said Ben emphatically.

"Maybe you'd better speak to Ernie, just in case," said Franklin, in a vain attempt to ease Margaret's mind.

Ben obediently picked up the phone and called Ernie's office. Jeanette answered, and it took a good two minutes for her to get Ernie connected with the telephone. Ben, Margaret and Franklin sipped their champagne in silence while they waited.

Finally, Ernie's voice could be heard on the other end, shouting at Jeanette.

"Next time, USE THE INTERCOM!" Then, in a calmer tone, "Hi Benny, what's up?"

"You won't have to say who produced the film, will you?" asked Ben, as much for Margaret's benefit as to get a reassurance from Ernie.

"No, of course not," Ernie said, as Ben held the phone out so Franklin and Margaret could hear the answer. "My responsibility is to defend the movie. It wouldn't make any sense to bring up who produced it now, would it?"

"No." said Ben. "but will you be putting Margaret on the stand?"

"Mrs. O'Leary? Don't worry. If she takes the stand, I'll handle her with kid gloves. Trust me."

Chapter 14

" All rise," said the bailiff. "The Superior Court of Suffolk County is now in session. The Honorable Judge Marian Wilcoxen presiding."

In a sign of the times, the Honorable Judge Marian Wilcoxen was one of those super-qualified Black women appointed as a political concession to appease two groups at once. This, of course, was not lost on the judge, who in reaction, ran an extremely tight ship. She was fair, bright, honest and tough. Depending on your own share of these qualities, you approached her courtroom with dread or delight.

Ernie couldn't have been happier with Marian Wilcoxen for this case, as he didn't see how he could lose it. After all, the odds were in his favor. It had been a long time since any film had been banned in Boston. The likelihood of any twelve jurors agreeing on a matter of taste was next to impossible. He sat by himself at the defendant's table, only half listening to Doug Finkel's opening statement.

"In conclusion, Your Honor," – everyone breathed a sigh of relief to hear that Doug was actually concluding – "let me say that we regret having to sully the court with such matters."

"Don't worry, Mr. Finkel," said Judge Wilcoxen, who underneath her tough demeanor also had a sense of humor.

"It's a dirty job, but somebody has to do it. Mr. McNerney, we'll hear your opening statement now."

Ernie rose, straightened his tie and tried to pull his suitcoat together over his middle.

"No opening statement at this time, Your Honor."

"Very well. Mr. Finkel, you may proceed," said Her Honor, as Ernie sat down again.

Doug first called Officer Connolly to recite the facts of the case, giving a brief overview of the film and establishing that the proper steps were taken in the raid. Then, a VCR and large monitor on a cart were wheeled in by a clerk and set up facing the jury.

"Your Honor," said Doug, "We now have the odious duty of displaying this film to the jury. You may wish to excuse yourself."

"I think I can take it, Mr. Finkel. The Court appreciates your concern," the judge responded with a bit of a smile at the young assistant DA's solicitousness.

"The Defense is also grateful for the Court's indulgence," said Ernie, half rising, then sitting again.

He leaned over to Doug at the Commonwealth's table.

"Wanna send out for popcorn?" he whispered.

"Disgusting," muttered Doug under his breath.

The lights in the courtroom were dimmed, and the clerk turned on the monitor and started the VCR. Some jurors seemed to be enjoying themselves. Others were clearly bored. One lady closed her eyes during the entire film, crossing herself and muttering, "Mother of God!" under her breath.

At the end of the film, the courtroom was quiet, except for the sound of one juror snoring. The judge rapped her gavel. "We're approaching the noon recess. I, for one, can use the lunch break after such a stimulating morning. Court is recessed until one o'clock."

Rapping her gavel again, Judge Marion Wilcoxen rose and quickly left the courtroom. The afternoon session began promptly at one o'clock, with the Commonwealth presenting its case first.

"Your Honor," began Doug, "the Commonwealth is not required to present evidence as to the artistic merit or lack thereof of this film. However, for the benefit of the jury, we would like to call just a few expert witnesses to give a critical and academic overview of this matter."

"Any objection, Mr. McNerney?" said Marion Wilcoxen from the bench.

"No, Your Honor. We too have our expert witnesses." "I imagined you would," sighed the judge. "You may proceed Mr. Finkel."

Then began the parade of "expert" witnesses, "designed to cancel each other out," as Franklin had predicted. Doug first called Dr. Seymour Malgren, professor of Contemporary Culture at Northeastern University, who taught the advanced seminar on the Philosophy of Cinema.

"Would you give us your professional opinion of this film, Dr. Malgren?" Doug asked.

"I may not be able to define hardcore pornography, but I know it when I see it, and we just saw it."

"Would you call it 'Art'?" asked Doug, in as objective a tone as he could summon.

"Absolutely not!"

Ernie's response to Dr. Malgren was Dr. Herbert Weisskopf, who gave the court a partial listing of his qualifications as an "expert."

"I was asked to give the first Marshall McLuhan lecture at the New School for Social Research in New York City. I was also a fellow at the Sorbonne in France, where I received special honors for my treatise on the metaphysics of the films of Jerry Lewis."

"Now, in the case of this film we saw this morning," said Ernie, "in your expert opinion, is it 'Art'?"

"Undoubtedly," answered the good Dr. Weisskopf. "The panache of an existential orgy in suburbia in this day and age ... it brought to mind the later work of Russ Meyer, particularly his use of color in *Beneath the Valley of the Ultra Vixens.*"

All in all, it was an entertaining afternoon of thrust and parry. Another of Doug's witnesses was Barbara Swazey, film critic for the *Boston Globe*, who also wrote the notes for the Institute of Contemporary Art's retrospective of great American industrial training films. She had actually refused to review *Adam and Eve and Rhonda and Joey,* on the grounds that it was "loathsome, vile and entirely too understandable."

"Understandable?" asked Ernie during cross-examination.

"Much too," said the critic. "Give me a good Italian art film any day, one that makes no sense unless some critic can explain it to the public. This is a film that ANYONE could figure out."

Then there was Ernie's Mr. Harold Morris, whose last book was *Twenty-Four Orgasms a Second: A History of Celluloid Sex.* To Mr. Morris, the movie was "a very important film, perhaps a seminal work. It's going to merit a special supplement when the paperback edition of my book comes out at Christmas."

And so on, through more "experts" saying, "Absolutely yes. I can't see where there would be any room for disagreement," or "Positively not, there isn't any question at all."

Finally, it was Ernie's turn to call his last witness. It came as a surprise.

"I call Mrs. Margaret O'Leary."

Margaret had been relieved when the assistant prosecutor had told her that her testimony was unnecessary, so she was caught completely off-guard. Trapped, she made her way uneasily to the stand and was sworn in.

"Please tell us what your position is with the anti-pornography group, Decency and Morality Now!" asked

Ernie, when the formalities were finished and Margaret had taken her seat.

"I'm the president," Margaret said, tentatively. She was wary of any questions Ernie might ask her.

"Your organization has taken a rather unusual interest in this film, has it not?" asked Ernie.

"I'm not sure what you mean," she answered, scanning the audience for help from Franklin and Ben.

"Perhaps I can help," said Ernie. "Over the past few months, you've personally picketed the BeauX Arts Cinema almost daily. And your organization has been outside there every day."

"Yes." Margaret was actually starting to sweat. *Where was he going with these questions?* she thought. *Was he going to expose the plot after all?*

"You've had the chance to observe the people who bought tickets to see the film, have you not?"

"Yes."

"And they were all the proverbial derelicts in dirty raincoats?" asked Ernie.

"No."

What is he doing? Margaret wondered. She wanted to scream, but somehow managed to keep her cool.

"No? How would you describe those people?"

"I'm sorry to say that a lot of them were young and professional-looking. Apparently, they had nothing better to do with their money ..."

"Did you see couples?"

"Yes," answered Margaret, more relaxed now.

Maybe this was all he wanted to know, after all, she thought. She didn't see what it had to do with anything, but she decided she would just answer the questions and hope for the best.

"So they could have been coming to see the movie on dates?"

"Some date! But yes, in the early evening, we would see men and women go in together."

"Mrs. O'Leary, you have just testified that a wide variety of people attended the film. Wouldn't you say that means the local community approves of this movie?"

"Maybe, it ..."

Margaret suddenly got her wits back about her.

"Of course not! It doesn't say anything of the kind!"

"On what basis are you contradicting your own sworn testimony?" said Ernie, moving in for the kill.

"I'm the president of Decency and Morality Now!"

Ernie walked back to the defense table, leaving Margaret feeling stranded on the stand.

"Yes," he finally said, "I believe you mentioned that."

"It's my job to know how the public feels about filthy movies like this one."

Ernie picked a folder up from his desk, opened it, and turned back toward Margaret.

"Mrs. O'Leary, it appears that your organization was on the verge of bankruptcy when you started protesting this film. Didn't you, in fact, start this campaign in order to save Decency and Morality ..."

Margaret, thinking Ernie was, in fact, going to spill the beans, panicked and jumped out of her seat, shouting, "Don't listen to him! It's all lies! You saw the movie yourselves!"

The courtroom erupted. Doug objected, the judge gaveled, the audience murmured, and Franklin and Ben jumped to their feet. Ernie just leaned against the defense table and smiled. Finally, the judge was able to restore order.

"Your Honor," said Ernie, apologetically, when the courtroom was again under control. "I merely wanted to suggest that the witness attacked a popular film to gain attention for her own failing organization. I had no idea she'd make an outburst like that. I have no further questions."

"Your Honor," Doug stood up, ready to launch into his own tirade.

Noticing that Margaret, still on the stand, was drying her eyes on a lace handkerchief, he simply stated, "I have no questions of this witness," and sat down again.

"At this time, the defense rests," said Ernie.

"I note the hour is late," said Her Honor. "We will adjourn until 10 a.m. tomorrow. It is my sincere hope that we can get this case to the jury by lunchtime. I trust this will not inconvenience counsel."

The look she gave Doug and Ernie indicated it would be in their best interest to hold their tongues.

"Court adjourned," said the Honorable Marian Wilcoxen, rapping her gavel.

Chapter 15

The Ninth Amendment Restaurant occupied the basement of one of the stately old buildings on Somerset, tucked away behind the courthouse. Off the well-beaten tourist trail, and too dark and old-world for the fern-bar crowd, it was frequented almost exclusively by lawyers and their clients.

The proprietors had gone to great lengths to provide the perfect environment for their particular patrons. A few tables stood alone in the center of the room. These were rarely used, and only in the event someone wanted to be seen, such as the need to establish an alibi. Most of the seating was in booths with high backs and sides. This was clearly a place for conducting private business.

Although the Ninth Amendment was only a few blocks from Louisburg Square, Franklin had never eaten there before. Whatever business he had conducted with lawyers in his lifetime had been in broad daylight, in well-lit offices. As he crossed the portal of the restaurant, he felt a rush of adrenaline. Just as he was actually starting to imagine himself in a Dashiell Hammett novel, the maître d' – who bore a striking resemblance to Raymond Burr – approached him.

"Good evening, sir. Are you Mr. Abbott?"

"I am," answered Franklin, trying not to seem surprised that he was identified by name here.

"Follow me, then, sir."

The maitre d' ushered Franklin to a dark corner booth, left a menu with him, and then discreetly withdrew.

"Thank you for taking the time to see me this evening," Franklin said to the man already seated in the booth.

"Glad to have the company," answered Ernie from the shadows across the table. "I had anticipated a longer session today, actually, so Marlene is expecting me to be eating in town."

"Good. I'd hate to keep you away from your family on my account."

Franklin opened the menu and looked down through the bottom of his bifocals.

"What do you recommend," he asked, clearly not yet ready to state his business.

"The specialty of the house is mako shark," answered Ernie, not bothering to open his own menu, but staring straight at Franklin who was "um-ing" and "ahuh-ing" while pretending to be interested in the bill of fare.

"Look," said Ernie finally. "I suppose you wanted to see me because of Margaret."

Franklin put down the menu and looked straight across at his dinner partner.

"Mr. McNerney, I appreciate the job you've been doing for us, particularly since I know how you feel about our cause, but was it really necessary to goad poor Margaret in that manner?"

It had been all Franklin and Ben could do to calm Margaret down after they left the courtroom. Fortunately, she had been too hysterical even to talk coherently or she might have spilled the beans entirely to the press. Franklin would have driven her right home, but his car was back at Louisburg Square. By the time they had walked from the courthouse to Cambridge Street to find a cab, Margaret had stopped hyperventilating, anyway. She just needed a good strong cup of tea in the comfort of her own home, she said, and would just as soon be alone.

After seeing Margaret off in a Town Taxi, Ben took his leave of Franklin and headed across the street for the Government Center T stop. Franklin decided a walk would do him good, so he turned to head back up Cambridge Street. He was mentally planning his route, thinking of taking Beacon Street and perhaps even strolling through that part of the Common, when he almost collided with Ernie. The attorney was coming out of the drugstore having just purchased the new *Boston Phoenix* with the cover story, "Porn – Beantown style."

Ernie's good spirits after Margaret's hysterics so annoyed Franklin that he asked for a word with him in private, whereupon the genial lawyer invited the Boston Brahmin to dinner. The two men agreed to meet at the Ninth Amendment, but decided it would be best to arrive there separately. Ernie started on ahead, while

Franklin remained behind, seeking a phone booth to call home and inform Martha he would be dining out that evening.

Now, sitting across from this man who was both colleague and adversary, Franklin had to actually force himself to remain polite.

"Frank," said Ernie in response to Franklin's reprimand, "You want me to save your movie, don't you? I'm doing the best I know how."

"You must be very proud of yourself, resorting to such tactics."

"It was all cheap theatrics, I know," Ernie admitted. "By all rights I never should have called her as a witness. If I had finished up with one of our so-called 'experts,' I would have left the jury confused. Instead, I gave them Margaret."

"I'm sorry," said Franklin, rising as if to leave.

"I didn't realize it was all just a game to you."

"Frank, wait a minute."

The serious tone of Ernie's voice was such a sudden change that Franklin found himself resuming his seat.

"I've been practicing law for more than fifteen years, and you know what? It IS all a game, and victory goes to the lawyer who can out-maneuver the others."

"Can I ask you something?" Ernie's sudden honesty gave Franklin an opening for a question he hadn't dared ask before.

"Shoot," Ernie responded.

"What satisfaction do you get from this? Another dirty movie goes free and you collect your money. Is that all it is to you?"

"I don't really care about these movies," said Ernie, with a sigh of relief that he could actually air his true feelings. "Sure, I get a kick out of watching them once in a while, because most of 'em are pretty funny. But you know how I justify my life's work to myself?"

"I'd be interested to hear," said Franklin, with a smile.

"I really believe in all that stuff about freedom of speech and freedom of the press. I know *Adam and Eve and Rhonda and Joey* isn't what the Founding Fathers had in mind when they wrote the First Amendment, but as long as I'm keeping the courts tied up with dirty movies rather than the *Boston Globe* or the *New York Times*, I can feel I've done my part."

"Then why are you helping us?" Franklin asked.

Ernie slumped back in the booth.

"Because much as I disagree with them, even your ideas have a right to be heard."

"You have children, don't you?"

"Yes, three boys," answered Ernie. "Why?"

"You say you disagree with us, but would you like to see your children exposed to these movies?"

"That's not the issue," said Ernie, sitting back up straight again in the booth, once more the avenging lawyer. "I don't want my kids to join the National Rifle Association either, but I'm not trying to have it outlawed."

"Then what is the issue? What can we do?"

Ernie just looked at him for a moment, then said simply, "I guess we COULD order dinner.'"

Feeling he had made his point in some small way, Franklin opened his menu. He was hungry, he discovered. *Nothing like an honest debate on a heated topic to give one an appetite,* he thought to himself. He did have to concede that Ernie had scored a point or two, and for the first time, he felt a twinge of doubt as to the righteousness of his own cause, and certainly the rightness of producing this film as a means of furthering it. But still the question remained – *what else could we do?*

Ernie didn't need to read the menu. He knew it by heart, and usually ordered the mako, anyway. *What more could I have said to Franklin*, he thought. He had built his career on the premise that there was no absolute right in the area of taste and propriety, and even if there were, absolute freedom would take precedence. Still, weren't he and Marlene taking great care to teach their boys to have respect for women and their own sexuality? Wasn't this really his own answer to Franklin's question?

The waiter approached the table and asked if the men had decided what to have.

"I'll have the mako, as usual," said Ernie. "Make that two," said Franklin.

While Ernie and Franklin were enjoying their mako, which tonight was broiled in a delicate red pepper sauce,

Ben was downing several cups of coffee in The Library. He had found the courtroom proceeding unnerving. Up until now, he had regarded the entire business as somewhat of a lark. He was even beginning to fancy himself alternately as a crusading knight-of-the-right or a hotshot movie producer. But in the intervals between these swings, a tiny suspicion began to grow that he was actually a sham, that be believed in neither and was losing himself somewhere in the mix.

So it was that Ben sat in The Library, trying to study, but unable to concentrate. His mind was whirling off in confusion as he drank coffee and looked at his watch. He was waiting for Joanne, and she was already an hour late, which was unlike her. When Joanne finally appeared, she was in high spirits.

"Sorry I'm late," she said, flinging herself down at Ben's table and flopping her backpack on top of his spread-out books. "I have some great news."

"I could use some about now," Ben said, clearing away his stuff to make room for hers. "What is it?"

Joanne was in such a good mood that she didn't even notice that Ben wasn't.

"All this publicity is getting me an interview for a real movie!"

"No kidding?" "Ben said, his own spirits rising a little in her presence.

"This is my big chance to get out of porno for good," she said. "To tell you the truth, I was beginning to have trouble facing myself in the mirror in the morning."

"You too?" Ben said, half under his breath, so it didn't completely register with Joanne.

"Yeah, I was even thinking of quitting, no matter what."

"I'm really glad, Joanne. What's the movie?"

"I don't want to say anything until it's sure."

Just at that moment, from across the room, came a voice calling, "Joanne! Hello there!" The two young people turned to see Professor Kingsley hustling toward them.

"Oh, my God ...!" Ben blurted out.

"It's all right," said Joanne, not realizing that Ben recognized the man as his Professor Dipso. "That's Professor Kingsley. He teaches my Meanings in Montage course."

"Good evening, Joanne," said Kingsley effusively, as he approached the table. Then, inspecting Ben closely, he asked, "Don't I know you from somewhere?"

"This is Ben Porter," said Joanne, "He's in the business school."

"Did you ever do any acting?" asked Kingsley, trying to puzzle out where he had seen Ben before.

"A little amateur theatrics ..." Ben volunteered, a bit nervously.

"Wait a minute, wait a minute," said Kingsley, stepping back and snapping his fingers. "Weren't you in *Inexhaustible?*"

Joanne, embarrassed, tried to change the subject.

"What brings you over here, Professor?"

"Oh, oh, yes. Are you up for that job at Slasher Productions?"

"Slasher Productions?" asked Ben, turning from Joanne to Kingsley, but being ignored by both.

"Yes," Joanne said, suddenly wary. "Why?"

"I got a call from them this afternoon. I told them you were one of my best students, that they'd be lucky to get you."

"Thank you," she said sincerely, relieved.

"Good luck with it, Joanne. I hope you get the job."

Turning to Ben, Kingsley shook his head.

"*Inexhaustible,* I'm sure of it. An incredible performance. A pleasure to meet you!"

After grabbing Ben's hand and shaking it to death, Kingsley gave a last smile to Joanne and was off.

"*Inexhaustible?*" said Ben, laughing.

"Don't ask," Joanne answered.

Chapter 16

"Ladies and gentlemen of the jury, in the end, I think you'll agree that the film is simply ninety minutes of animals in heat."

Doug was concluding his spellbinding summation to the jury the next morning. As he spoke, he felt the full force of his words crashing on each jury member, penetrating their thoughts, leaving no doubt in their minds as to the moral rectitude of his position.

"We see them not as PEOPLE but as BODIES," Doug continued, giving it all the drama he could muster, punching up certain words while he looked each juror in the eye in turn. Ah yes, he was thinking, as he paused briefly for effect, the power he held. This is why he went to law school, to right the wrongs of the world.

"I ask that you declare what you've seen with YOUR OWN EYES: this film is OBSCENE, and the people of Suffolk County should be spared any further exposure to its POISONING influence. Thank you for your patience and understanding through this distasteful matter."

With a scornful look at Ernie, Doug triumphantly crossed back to his table and took his seat.

Then it was Ernie's turn. He gave an eloquent plea for the First Amendment, arguing that it protected even those artforms at the outer limits of good taste. He ended with a simple appeal to the jurors' own rights.

"As you go into that jury room, let me leave you with but one question: is there anyone, anywhere in the world, who you would trust to decide FOR YOU what you can read or watch? Then, after you've decided that question, I ask you to decide for the defendant. Thank you."

Judge Marian Wilcoxen then gave her instructions to the jury, rapped her gavel, and the twelve honorable men and women chosen to sit in judgment on the case retired to begin their deliberations.

Margaret, Ben and Franklin filed out of the courtroom. As they stood in the hallway, trying to decide whether to go out for lunch, go back to the office, or sit and await the jury's decision, Doug approached them.

"You handled yourself very well on the stand yesterday, Mrs. O' Leary," he said.

"Thank you, Mr. Finkel, Margaret replied warmly. She liked this young man. He reminded her of her cousin Bridgit's third boy.

"I've enjoyed watching you work, as well," said Franklin to the beaming Assistant District Attorney.

"Why thank you," Doug said effusively. "With the jury out, we should have time for lunch. Would you care to join me?"

"What a delightful idea," said Margaret.

But just as they reached the front door of the courthouse, Albert came running full speed up to them.

"The jury's reached a verdict!" he panted.

"In fifteen minutes?" said Doug, consulting his watch. "I guess lunch will have to wait."

"How could they have decided so soon," asked Ben, as they all rushed back to the courtroom.

"What could it mean?" added Margaret.

"I'm not sure, Mrs. O'Leary," said Doug, trying not to look concerned. "We'd better get back inside."

The courtroom was hushed as people filed back in. Judge Wilcoxen brought the proceedings straight to the point, within the confines of the usual court rituals.

"Have you reached a verdict?" said the judge, as soon as the preliminaries were completed.

"We have, Your Honor," said the foreman.

"And how does the jury find?"

"Guilty, Your Honor," said the foreman.

The Courtroom was eerily quiet. Everyone was simply too stunned to move or speak. The foreman looked around, puzzled by the silence.

"We thought it was obvious," he added, with a nervous twitch.

By the time the principals in this courtroom drama gathered their things together and made their way down the stairs and out the front door of the courthouse, word of the verdict had reached the media. The scene, which inside had been too quiet, gave way to chaos outside, as reporters grabbed anyone and everyone in a feeding frenzy for sound bites.

In one circle of microphones, Ernie was telling TV news:

"I'm saddened by this verdict, but we will appeal. We look at this as a temporary setback for free expression, with the emphasis on the word 'temporary.'"

A radio reporter for WGBH spotted Margaret being half-carried out by Franklin and Ben.

"Mrs. O'Leary, how are you enjoying the victory?"

"I'm shocked," muttered Margaret. "I can't believe they did it!"

Meanwhile, Tim Willard was doing a stand-up on the courthouse steps. He held a mike up to Doug, who was practically reeking of the sweet smell of victory:

"I think today's decision is a warning to the filth-mongers that a new day is dawning in Boston. The people have said, ENOUGH!"

Tim congratulated him, thanked him, and then completed his piece with, "Who knows, we may be seeing the birth of a new political career as well. Already there is talk of having young Doug Finkel seek his boss's job in the upcoming elections."

Elsewhere in the building, watching all this on TV, was Burton Halloran. He was not happy. Indeed, he was screaming, "ALBERT!!!" at the top of his lungs.

When the reporters had finally run off to edit their stories, Ben, Margaret and Franklin shared a cab back to the D.A.M.N.! office. Their unexpected "victory" in court had only made them bewildered and depressed.

"I don't understand it," said Margaret when they were finally seated with cups of tea and coffee. "For years we try to clean up this town, and we get laughed at almost to bankruptcy. And when we count on them to treat OUR film like every other, THEN thy go and get religion."

"I can't figure out this world anymore," Franklin added. "Who can make sense of it?"

"Look on the bright side," offered Ben. "At least we aren't in jail."

"True," Franklin replied. "But with the legal fees for defending the film, we've fallen further into the red than before."

They all fell silent, each one wondering what it had all been for, and just what WAS the meaning of life, anyway. Someone knocked on the door, and Ben jumped up to answer it. His spirits brightened when he saw Joanne standing there, even though she looked terribly upset.

"I just heard the news on the radio," she said. "I can't believe it!"

"Neither can we," said Ben, as he ushered her into the office and closed the door.

"Excuse me, Ben. "I don't believe we know your friend."

"You must be Margaret," said Joanne, extending her hand to the other woman. "I'm Joanne Taylor."

Margaret started to take the offered hand, but pulled away when Joanne added, "I made your movie."

"But you're a young lady!" said Franklin.

"I suppose it doesn't matter anymore," said Ben. "J. Thomas is a BU film student who's been supporting herself making films like ours."

"But that's terrible!" Margaret exclaimed.

"I agree with you now," said Joanne, "But it was the only way I could work. But thanks to your project, I've been able to get a legitimate assignment at last. I can assure you, my porno days are over for good."

"You got it!" Ben exclaimed, hugging her.

"That's wonderful!" said Margaret. "So some good will come out of this, after all."

"And Ben," said Joanne, "I hope you won't mind but I've offered your services as associate producer."

"What?"

"I told them how well we worked together on this film ..."

"But I don't know anything about the movie business ... and I have a job."

"Silly, you're getting an MBA. This is just another business. Besides, you don't think I'd do it without you, do you?"

"Franklin, I ..." Ben turned to the older man, not sure what to do or say.

"Don't be foolish, Ben," said Franklin. "Take it. We don't know what the future holds for us here, anyway."

Ben took Joanne's hands in his.

"How can I resist?" he said, and kissed her.

"You see, Franklin," said Margaret, beaming at the sight of the young lovers. "Love does triumph over all."

"What's this new movie going to be about?" Franklin asked, when Ben and Joanne had taken a breather and joined them at the table.

"It's a horror film," Joanne explained. "I brought along a poster for it."

"That was fast," said Ben, as Joanne got up to retrieve the poster she had left by the door.

"With this kind of film, they do the advertising campaign first, THEN they make the movie to go with it."

"*Blender*," Franklin read from the poster. "The most frightening movie since *The Texas Chainsaw Massacre* .... No one will be admitted during the horrifying PUREE sequence." Lowering the poster, he said, "That sounds delightful," in a voice trying hard not to offend.

"At least it's good clean fun," said Margaret brightly.

"Congratulations, Ms. Taylor," said Franklin sincerely. "I'm glad SOMEONE was able to profit from this episode. I, for one, am glad it's over."

"Think of it," said Joanne. "The first film banned in Boston in more than twenty-five years. It's quite an achievement in its own right!"

"Who knows what it may mean?" said Margaret.

They all just looked at each other, trying to figure out what it actually DID mean in the great scheme of things.

Suddenly, Ben smiled. And then he laughed.

"What it means," he said, "is now that we're banned in Boston, we're going to run forever in New York!"

Blender had been playing for several months in New York when Joanne and Ben ventured down to The Big Apple. They stood in the middle of Times Square and enjoyed watching the line form outside the theater that was playing their movie.

Just around the corner, in front of another theater with long lines, a marquee announced, *Adam and Eve and Rhonda and Joey*. It was hard to read the title, because across the top, in bright red letters, a huge sign declared, "BANNED IN BOSTON, 27th BIG MONTH!"

Deborah Hand-Cutler is a writer and musician living in Tehachapi, CA. She started her writing career in New York and Boston, working in print, radio and media. She has written plays produced by the Tehachapi Community Theatre, and served on the City Council and as mayor of that city. She and her husband, Peter Cutler, own Fiddlers Crossing, a concert venue in  Tehachapi. They both are part of Folkscene, a radio program that has been on the air for over 50 years. She also teaches cello and mountain dulcimer. Her first novel, *The Snake in the Garden*, deals with racism in Arkansas during the twentieth century. It was written in collaboration with Brenda Sutton Turner, a former Motown artist who grew up under Jim Crow laws in Texarkana, Arkansas.

Daniel M. Kimmel is a veteran Boston-based film critic and author. His film reviews currently appear at NorthShoreMovies.net. He also writes on classic SF films for "Space and Time" magazine. He is the 2018 recipient of the Skylark Award, given by the New England Science Fiction Association. He was a finalist for a  Hugo Award for *Jar Jar Binks Must Die… and other observations about science fiction movies,* and for the Compton Crook Award for best first novel for *Shh! It's a Secret: a novel about Aliens, Hollywood, and the Bartender's Guide.* He is the author of *Time on My Hands: My Misadventures in Time Travel.* and *Father of the Bride of Frankenstein.*

Made in the USA
Middletown, DE
16 July 2022

69513246R00099